Johanna ... *this could hardly* ...

Some guy buying you ice cream out of gratitude for saving his kid's life wasn't a date, now was it?

Maybe she was reading too much into this.

Wasn't it possible that Hunter was simply a toucher? You know, not touchy-feely in a bad kind of way, just...tactile. Who knew? Maybe he kissed everybody goodbye. For all she knew, he might have some French blood in his heritage. Then it wouldn't be a first date kind of kiss, but just a social kind of thing. The French were always kissing each other.

Johanna angled her head to better meet Hunter's kiss. She'd never been kissed by a Frenchman....

Dear Reader,

Silhouette's 20th anniversary celebration continues this month in Romance, with more not-to-be-missed novels that take you on the romantic journey from courtship to commitment.

First we revisit STORKVILLE, USA, where a jaded Native American rancher seems interested in *His Expectant Neighbor*. Don't miss this second book in the series by Susan Meier! Next, *New York Times* bestselling author Kasey Michaels returns to the lineup, launching her new miniseries, THE CHANDLERS REQUEST.... One bride, *two* grooms—who will end up *Marrying Maddy*? In *Daddy in Dress Blues* by Cathie Linz, a Marine embarks on his most terrifying mission—fatherhood!—with the help of a pretty preschool teacher.

Then Valerie Parv whisks us to a faraway kingdom as THE CARRAMER CROWN continues. *The Princess's Proposal* puts the lovely Adrienne and her American nemesis on a collision course with...love. The ever-delightful Terry Essig tells the tale of a bachelor, his orphaned brood and the woman who sparks *A Gleam in His Eye*. Shhh.... We can't give anything away, but you *must* learn *The Librarian's Secret Wish*. Carol Grace knows...and she's anxious to tell you!

Next month, look for another installment of STORKVILLE, USA, and THE CHANDLERS REQUEST...from *New York Times* bestselling author Kasey Michaels. Plus, Donna Clayton launches her newest miniseries, SINGLE DOCTOR DADS!

Happy Reading!

Mary-Theresa Hussey

Mary-Theresa Hussey
Senior Editor

Please address questions and book requests to:
Silhouette Reader Service
· U.S.: 3010 Walden Ave., P.O. Box 1325, Buffalo, NY 14269
Canadian: P.O. Box 609, Fort Erie, Ont. L2A 5X3

A Gleam in His Eye

TERRY ESSIG

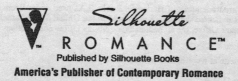

Silhouette

R O M A N C E™

Published by Silhouette Books

America's Publisher of Contemporary Romance

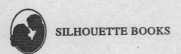

SILHOUETTE BOOKS

RECYCLED PAPER

ISBN 0-373-19472-2

A GLEAM IN HIS EYE

Copyright © 2000 by Mary Therese Essig

Visit Silhouette at www.eHarlequin.com

Printed in U.S.A.

Books by Terry Essig

Silhouette Romance

House Calls #552
The Wedding March #662
Fearless Father #725
Housemates #1015
Hardheaded Woman #1044
Daddy on Board #1114
Mad for the Dad #1198
What the Nursery Needs... #1272
The Baby Magnet #1435
A Gleam in His Eye #1472

Silhouette Special Edition

Father of the Brood #796

TERRY ESSIG

says that writing is her escape valve from a life that leaves very little time for recreation or hobbies. With a husband and six young children, Terry works on her stories a little at a time, between seeing to her children's piano, sax and trombone lessons, their gymnastics, ice skating and swim team practices, and her own activities of leading a Brownie troop, participating in a car pool and attending organic chemistry classes. Her ideas, she says, come from her imagination and her life—neither one of which is lacking!

IT'S OUR 20th ANNIVERSARY!
We'll be celebrating all year,
Continuing with these fabulous titles,
On sale in September 2000.

Intimate Moments

#1027 Night Shield
Nora Roberts

#1028 Night of No Return
Eileen Wilks

#1029 Cinderella for a Night
Susan Mallery

#1030 I'll Be Seeing You
Beverly Bird

#1031 Bluer Than Velvet
Mary McBride

#1032 The Temptation of Sean MacNeill
Virginia Kantra

Special Edition

#1345 The M.D. She Had To Marry
Christine Rimmer

#1346 Father Most Wanted
Marie Ferrarella

#1347 Gray Wolf's Woman
Peggy Webb

#1348 For His Little Girl
Lucy Gordon

#1349 A Child on the Way
Janis Reams Hudson

#1350 At the Heart's Command
Patricia McLinn

Desire

#1315 Slow Waltz Across Texas
Peggy Moreland

#1316 Rock Solid
Jennifer Greene

#1317 The Next Santini Bride
Maureen Child

#1318 Mail-Order Cinderella
Kathryn Jensen

#1319 Lady with a Past
Ryanne Corey

#1320 Doctor for Keeps
Kristi Gold

Romance

#1468 His Expectant Neighbor
Susan Meier

#1469 Marrying Maddy
Kasey Michaels

#1470 Daddy in Dress Blues
Cathie Linz

#1471 The Princess's Proposal
Valerie Parv

#1472 A Gleam in His Eye
Terry Essig

#1473 The Librarian's Secret Wish
Carol Grace

Chapter One

"All right, you guys," swim coach Johanna Durbin yelled at her bedraggled, dripping group of eight-year-olds and unders. "Now you pay for that last horrendous set of freestyle. Everybody get your sticks. It's time to beat a few bottoms."

What? Hunter Pace soared to his feet. The transition from uncle to parent had been recent for him, and times had certainly changed since he was a kid, but he was fairly certain physical contact was illegal. Even if it wasn't, nobody, nowhere, no how and no matter how good-looking was touching a member of his new family with a stick. Suddenly he was very glad he'd decided to stick around and watch his niece and nephew's swim practice.

Hunter started moving but paused at the end of his bench in the bleacher stand. None of the kids looked upset. Sure, they were groaning and complaining, but they all headed for their swim bags with next to no foot-dragging, and returned to the pool's side, foot-long chunks of dowel rod in hand.

"You beat Matt last week, Coach Jo. Can it be my turn today?" one little darling dared to tease.

"Beat Billy, Coach Jo. He cutted in front of me again."

"Nuh-uh" came the immediate denial.

"Uh-uh."

"I gotta go to the bathroom," contributed one child, legs crossed and hand pressed firmly between her legs. Johanna waved her toward the locker room.

"Beat the new kids. Maybe it'll make them swim faster."

Hunter half rose again.

"Marcus," said Coach Jo, "you know the rules. No put-downs. Karen and Robby just started swim team. They'll get faster all by themselves as they practice, just like you did. I think maybe I'll beat you instead."

Yeah, thought Hunter. Beat the little jerkface, picking on his niece and nephew like that.

But the little jerkface danced out of Coach Jo's reach. "Gotta catch me first," he said, and dived into the pool. "Besides, you just *pretended* to beat Billy. He told me so," Marcus added when his head cleared the surface.

"Oh, yeah?" Coach Jo asked. "Watch this." She grabbed the child next to her, who happened to be her little sister, flipped her upside down and lightly tapped her seat while making loud smacking sounds.

The kids all laughed, including the victim. "I'm telling Mom," the small fry said.

Johanna fell willingly into the trap. "Oh, no, don't do that, Aubrey. Don't tell Mom on me. I'll do anything to make it up to you. How about an extra piece of my birthday cake come Friday?"

Five other youngsters pressed close.

"I'll let you beat me, Coach Jo, if you bring me a piece of your birthday cake."

"What kind is it going to be?" another one wanted to know before committing himself.

"Chocolate."

"How old you gonna be, Coach Jo?"

"Old," Jo's little sister replied. "Really old." She danced back out of Johanna's reach. "Twenty-five. My mom says that's three times as old as us guys."

"Man," a little blonde said reverently. "That *is* old."

Hunter eavesdropped shamelessly, calmer as he saw the coach in action. Twenty-five, hmm? Only a few years younger than he. Hunter wasn't yet sure if he totally approved of the blond dynamo, but he was a desperate man and becoming more so with every passing day. He couldn't help but notice Coach Jo's bare left hand.

This was a new sensation for Hunter. He enjoyed women, certainly. What wasn't there to enjoy about them? The opposite sex was delightful with their softer curves and interesting, um, shaping. And their minds! Well their minds were a fascinating foreign landscape a man could travel forever and never quite be able to map out. Oh, yes, Hunter loved them dearly, each and every puzzling one, but he'd never been much interested in attaching himself permanently to one. In fact, up to now, he'd avoided marriage at all costs. Whenever he dated a woman, he kept a careful watch for signs of nesting. If she started detouring him through the baby section during a harmless stroll through the local department store and investigating the local school system in his neighborhood, he knew he had to end the relationship—or risk losing his bachelor freedom. Hunter just hadn't been ready for marriage or family. Until now.

Hunter sighed. Unfortunately, through absolutely no fault of his own, things had changed and he found himself with a bad case of *ready or not, here they come*. Hunter needed a woman in his life. He needed a mother for his brood. His niece and nephews were now his, permanent, full-time for the next fifteen to twenty years. His big brother was up there somewhere laughing at him, he just knew it. "I hope you're enjoying yourself," he muttered to the heavens.

"But I'll be joining you someday myself, probably a lot sooner than I ever thought if your kids have their way, and I will get my payback. See if I don't."

When his brother and sister-in-law had died in that accident, leaving Hunter their four children to raise, he'd been so naively sure he could handle things by himself. How hard could it be to throw food in front of the little miscreants a few times a day and send them up to bed at eight-thirty every night?

Hard. His recently acquired crew of four had spent the last month and a half proving just how hard it could be. Because of their recent loss, the kids had trouble letting Hunter out of their sight, trouble sleeping in the dark, trouble...just lots of trouble. Hunter needed help and he was becoming desperate enough to admit it.

Now, when he was finally ready to be caught, the women of his acquaintance all seemed to have done an abrupt about-face. It wasn't really a change of heart, the last one had earnestly assured him. Certainly she wanted children—her own. Elaine simply hadn't been ready to take on *four* of somebody else's before she'd even taken her own genetic code down from the shelf and dusted it off.

Hunter nodded thoughtfully as he observed. Now, this young lady seemed to actually enjoy young children. Why or how he couldn't begin to imagine. It's not as if kids could discuss the Cubs latest trade or the stock trends with you. But then, as he'd noticed more than once before, the female mental landscape was one confusing place. Hunter shook his head and tuned back into the other apparently delicate matter of Coach Jo's age.

"Thanks a lot, Aubrey." Johanna glared at her sister. "All right, big mouth, now you're in for it."

"Chocolate frosting, too?"

"With sprinkles," Johanna confirmed, her attention momentarily diverted from her unable-to-keep-anything-secret younger sibling.

"I guess you could beat me," one more said after brief consideration. "So long as the sprinkles are chocolate, too."

"Too late to take it back," Aubrey said with a smirk. "She already promised me the extra cake and I decided not to tell."

"I just may tell Mom myself what a little con artist you've become, young lady." Then Johanna hugged her. "Oh, well, a deal's a deal. All right, everybody in the water. Do a good job and I just might bring cupcakes for everybody. Ten fifties freestyle stroke drill on the one-twenty. Watch the pace clock." Johanna turned to study the large poolside clock. "All right," she said as the second hand approached the top of the clock. "Ready and... go."

Hunter Pace watched his seven-year-old niece and eight-year-old nephew look around in confusion. He didn't blame them. Any attempts at poolside order and organization were well hidden. It was his children's first session ever with a swim team, and the energetic and incredibly vivacious coach seemed to be speaking Greek. He rose, prepared to go question Coach Jo on the directions and decipher them for Karen and Robby. Truth be told, he wouldn't mind getting close to the kids' new coach again. Her coaching style seemed a bit unorthodox to him, but anybody who exuded the natural sex appeal Coach Johanna exuded got the benefit of his doubt. He'd make it a point to keep an eye on her, that was all. The closer eye the better. Coach Johanna was not only a looker, she smelled like a ripe peach. Hunter had discovered that interesting tidbit when he'd introduced Karen, Robby and himself at the beginning of the session. He'd always had a thing for peaches. And fruits were, after all, an important part of any man's diet.

But before he could even rise to his full six foot two, he realized it would be once again unnecessary for him to interfere and sat back down. His thighs were really getting a workout what with all this standing up and sitting down.

He could probably leave the leg sets out of his regime later on that night.

Coach Johanna already had her arms around his niece and nephew while she instructed them as to what she wanted them to do. Then she handed them each a twelve-inch length of thick dowel rod and gestured at the children swimming in the pool, as she pointed out the correct way to use the sticks for the freestyle drill. She pointed out the large clock propped up by the pool's side and explained that ten fifties meant swimming fifty yards, or to one end of the pool and back, ten times.

Karen and Robby nodded seriously several times, their little chests heaving from all the exertion. Maybe they should sit down. He was trying to wear them out so he could get them to bed at a decent time, not kill them. Once again Hunter got up to interfere, and once again found it unnecessary. He was starting to feel like a jack-in-the-box. He watched while Johanna directed Robby and Karen to sit on the edge of the pool, where they kicked their feet in the water and called out times from the clock as kids came in and hit the wall.

Never turning her back to the water, Johanna began picking up kickboards from around the pool's edge and stacking them neatly. Positioning herself so that the swimmers were always in her sight presented her backside to the gallery, giving Hunter a view he greatly appreciated.

After the first two sets, Johanna took Robby and Karen over to the slowest lane and had them slide in. She walked along the edge of the pool beside them, encouraging them as they tried to copy the other children, holding the rod out in front of them while they stroked one arm, grabbed the rod with that hand, then rotated the other arm.

"Stretch out," Johanna yelled. "That's it, reach for it. Now kick. Kick, kick, kick! Good job. Put your face in the water and only turn your head to breathe every third stroke.

That a way! You're going to be awesome swimmers, I can already tell.''

Hunter swelled with newly acquired parental pride. Of course they'd be awesome. Why just look at them, they were like little fish out there, obviously in their element. His eyes narrowed in contemplation. Just exactly what kind of credentials did this young swim coach have? She obviously could recognize pure talent when she saw it, but beyond that? Karen and Robby should have the best, after all. Just look how quickly they caught on—see how they hung on to that stick? Neither one had dropped it yet. Well, anyone that coordinated could very easily have Olympic potential.

Johanna handed out stopwatches at the end of the set and walked the youngsters through taking their own pulse. She doubted any of them were even close to getting the correct rate, but eventually it would click in and they'd be able to do it. And it made them feel like big shots, keeping their interest level high. She didn't want any eight-year-old burn-outs, which was why she tried to vary the practices and keep everything low-key and nonthreatening. This practice, however, had been uncomfortable for her. She'd never really quite found her groove. There'd been two new kids, cute but without a whole heck of a lot of natural athletic ability. Johanna certainly recognized that not everyone would go to the Olympics or even swim collegially, and in general, she disliked that elitist attitude so many sport enthusiasts took—her student Marcus and his parents a case in point. You didn't have to have Olympic potential to benefit from and enjoy a good, wholesome sport. Exercise was good for everyone, after all. And with a lot of work those two new little water sprites might be good enough to at least swim competitively during high school, maybe even earn a letter.

No, the kids weren't the problem.

It was the dad.

He'd stared at her almost the whole time until she'd wanted to stop and make sure she didn't have her shorts on inside out or backward. Heck, he was *still* staring at her. She'd been doing this for a million years and he had her feeling self-conscious. She *never* felt self-conscious. Well, at least not much anymore. Johanna did not appreciate the fact that this man she didn't even know could make her feel that way now.

Johanna blew her whistle. "Okay, my little munchkins, that's it for tonight. I need all my stopwatches back in my box, the kickboards and pull buoys back in their bins, and I need everybody to take all their stuff home with them. Next pair of goggles I pick up off the deck are mine. I could use a nice new pair. Anybody who leaves their swimsuit in the locker room loses it. I'm wearing it next time."

That got a good laugh.

"Coach Jo, you couldn't wear our swimsuits. They're too little."

"Oh, yeah? Maybe I'll put one on each leg and one on each arm, ever think of that? And I'd have enough to do it, too, if last practice was any indication. If I wanted to be a maid I'd have gone to maid school. Make sure you've got everything before you leave. No more upset parental phone calls, hear me?"

They all nodded agreement between smiles and giggles at the mental image of their coach piecing together all their suits to create one of her own.

"It'd never work," one whispered.

"Yeah, it'd fall right apart to pieces."

"I dunno. They're real stretchy."

"She could use lots and lots of safety pins. My mom's got a whole big box. She says they're just as good as sewing."

Johanna shook her head. "You're all hopeless. Okay, guys, scram. See you tomorrow."

At least now the man would leave. Most of the parents

congregated out in front of the locker room and chatted while waiting for their swimmers to shower and dress.

Hunter decided not to exit with the rest of the herd of parents who'd come to watch the practice. He wanted to talk to the coach, but he wasn't quite sure how to approach her. Robby and Karen had not come to blows, verbal or otherwise, with each other. That could only mean they'd been engrossed in what they'd been doing and had had a good time.

This was good.

It was better than good. It was wonderful, unexpected, marvelous. This bit of manna from heaven was courtesy of Johanna, unorthodox though she may be. She had entertained and worn out those two. Any sleep he got tonight was due to this wonderful woman. He owed her. It was only right that he should repay her with maybe a drink or even a meal out, right? It certainly wouldn't be any strain to go out with her. Hunter would take her someplace decent and see to it she had a good time. He could do that. He was cool. At least he had been until his entire world had caved in. Maybe he'd pick her brain a bit and—see. Karen and Robby took forever in the morning to dress. This would probably be no different. He had time. He could talk to her now.

Oh, God, he wasn't leaving. Why didn't he leave? Johanna unbuttoned her shirt and stepped out of her shorts.

Hunter, who'd been about to rise for the umpteen millionth time, froze. Good Lord, she was taking her clothes off. Right there on deck, she was taking them off. What was the woman thinking of? There were young children around. Hell, *he* was around, and Hunter wasn't sure his heart was up to the havoc Johanna Durbin's disrobing was causing his system.

Hunter was both relieved and disappointed when he realized Johanna wore a racing suit under her apparel.

And he'd thought she'd been a looker before, with her petite stature, blond curls and large, soulful eyes.

Competitive swimsuits were notoriously unflattering. They mashed a woman's breasts flat and hugged the body, unerringly delineating every flaw in a mean-spirited, merciless, unforgiving display. Well, if this was Johanna's body displayed at its worst, he didn't even need to see her best. The body her suit outlined was flawless. Really. The woman didn't have any flab, at least none Hunter could detect. No indeed, Johanna Durbin's body needed no mercy or forgiveness.

She'd just risen above looker in his estimation and had levitated several degrees to stunner.

Hunter's mouth actually began to water. How ridiculous. Surely at his age he was beyond all that. He was too urbane, too with it for such an elementary response to a female.

Still, he had to swallow.

Hunter shook his head to clear it. "Get a grip," he ordered himself. He rose, determined to go and talk to the woman. "Damn the physiological responses," he mumbled. "Full speed ahead."

"Oh, God, he's coming over here," Johanna whispered. A new and decidedly odd feeling uncurled in the pit of her stomach. This was a dangerous man. Something deep inside of her recognized that fact. Johanna wanted nothing to do with him. He'd introduced himself earlier, but Johanna had evidently blocked his name out, for she couldn't come up with it right then. It didn't matter. For her, his name was spelled *Trouble*. Married, divorced, whatever, he had kids and she was within a few weeks of being done with all responsibility to that particular breed. Footloose and fancy-free. That was going to be her.

Johanna quickly swung around, pretending she hadn't noticed his approach. Quickly, she stuffed her blond tresses up under her cap and pulled a pair of goggles into place. She dived off the edge.

Hunter stopped and watched her lithe form eat up the water. It was obvious Robby and Karen's new coach had swum competitively. He didn't know all that much about swimming, but he knew grace when he saw it. Johanna displayed an economy of form that was beautiful to watch. There were no wasted motions, no twisting, no struggling. She had executed what certainly looked like a beautiful flip turn at the far end of the pool and returned to her starting point in what he was sure was less than half a minute. Johanna flipped again and steamed away.

"Where's the fire?" Hunter asked her wake.

"Uncle Hunter, what're you doin' still here? Everybody else is out in front. Me and Robby was looking and looking for you."

Hunter reached down and rested a hand on Karen's still-wet head. "Were you, pumpkin?" Then, recognizing fear when he heard it, Hunter said, "Well, you found me. I'll always be here for you. Mommy and Daddy would have been, too, if they'd had a choice, sweetie." His brother and sister-in-law's death had shaken their children's little world pretty badly and Hunter knew it would take a lifetime of reassurances to fix the damage.

Karen studied him with a serious eye, before nodding once. "Okay. Hold on, I gotta go tell Robby I found you. Robby!" Karen bellowed, and took off at a run.

Hunter gave one last lingering look to the pool and its sole occupant and slowly followed in Karen's wake.

Several more adults showed up for adult lap time and Johanna wove her way through them, pushing herself hard for the next hour. By the time she pulled herself out of the pool, body exhausted but her mind still revved, her almost-eighteen-year-old brother Charlie had long since stopped by and taken home Aubrey and three more siblings; ten-year-old Stephen and nine-year-old William, who'd been swimming with the nine- and ten-year-old group, along with thirteen-year-old Grace, who'd worked with a third even older group. Johanna headed for the locker room, showered the chlorine off, dressed and drove herself home. Tucking her car into the garage for the night, she lovingly patted its hood as she passed in front of it. Her eyes started scanning the moment she left the garage.

"Good. Christopher took me seriously about doing a better job cutting the grass," she acknowledged to herself as she passed through the yard and entered the house through the back door.

"Looks like the dishes are done and it's possible the floor may have been swept." Johanna opened the refrigerator door. "Lunches made." She closed the door, went to the bottom of the steps to the second floor and yelled, "Homework check! Bring your assignment notebooks and matching papers down to the kitchen! Aubrey?"

"Yeah?"

"Did you practice?"

"Yeah."

"Uh-huh. Anybody hear you practice that would be willing to bear witness?"

"William said I had to say he'd practiced, too, otherwise he was gonna say I didn't, either, but I really did. You can even ask."

"Charlie?" Johanna yelled.

"All right, okay, I'll turn it off. Man, you have radar ears. How'd you even know I had the television on while I studied?"

She hadn't. "I know all and see all. Did Aubrey practice?"

"Yeah."

"For more than five minutes?"

Charlie didn't respond right away. Evidently he had to think about it. "Maybe," he finally responded.

"Close enough," Johanna muttered, too tired to pursue it any further. She went out to the kitchen table and began to check homework assignments. After a few minutes, she sat back and eyed her four youngest siblings, who stood waiting for her to finish.

"Pretty good, guys. William, this one paper needs to be rewritten more neatly, but other than that, you all did a great job."

Johanna glanced around the kitchen, noted the cookie sheet in the sink. "Did Chris bake the cookies?"

They all nodded.

"Peanut butter. But he wouldn't let us have none," Aubrey complained. "Said he was keeping them all for himself."

"He was teasing, honey. They're for lunches. But you know, you all did such a great job at swimming and getting your work done I think we should break out the milk and all have a cookie."

"Yes!" Grace pumped her fist and raced for the milk, Stephen got the glasses and Aubrey climbed on a chair to reach the cookie tin while William hurriedly rewrote his paper in better handwriting. Johanna knew for a fact it still wasn't his personal best, but decided not to push it. She was too tired and the end of the school year was too close.

Sixteen-year-old Christopher ambled in during their treat. "Where's Mom?" he asked, snagging a cookie.

"I was gonna have that one," William immediately complained.

"Then you should have been quicker," Chris informed Will while holding the cookie out of his reach. "Besides, I'm the one who made them." He bit into it.

Johanna shook her head. "Mom had a late meeting," she explained. "Probably will every night this week. She's got a big deal cooking."

Chris snorted. "What else is new? She's never home."

"Be grateful," Johanna said. "Things could have gotten really rocky after Dad died if she hadn't been able to make a success of herself. And she's a whole lot tougher than me. Why, I remember when I was your age…"

Aubrey edged closer to her big sister. "Jo?"

"Yeah, honey?"

"Those two new kids at swim practice? They came to school today, too. One of them is going to be in my class. I kinda liked them."

"Did you? Good. Me, too. And it's hard to be the new kid, so they'll need you to be nice to them."

"Yeah, only know what?"

"What?"

"That guy?"

"What guy?"

"The guy what brought them."

"Their dad? What about him?"

"He *looked* like a dad, only he wasn't."

Johanna's ears perked up. "He wasn't their dad?"

"Nuh-uh. They kept calling him Uncle Hunter, so I asked Karen why and they said it was 'cuz that's what he was. Their uncle."

Aubrey now had Johanna's total attention. "Oh, really?"

"Yeah. Everybody was yelling and stuff in the locker room and I still had some water in my ears so I couldn't hear too good what she was saying, but it was something about their parents going someplace and them staying with their uncle."

Well, well, well, wouldn't it be nice if her instincts had been off base? Easily over six feet with dark, dark hair and piercing blue eyes, this particular man fit her definition of the quintessential male. In fact, you could probably look up the word *male* in the dictionary and find *Hunter Pace* listed as the definition. "So he only has the kids temporarily," Johanna murmured out loud.

Aubrey scrunched her thin little shoulders. "I guess. Know what else? They got two more in their family. Aaron and Mikie. Karen says it's no fair 'cuz she's the only girl."

Johanna watched Christopher finish off the milk directly from the gallon container. Boys were so…primitive. "I can see her point. Rinse that out and put it in the recycling container, Chris," she directed her brother, and sat back in her chair. "I wonder why they changed schools and everything?" she mused out loud, then shrugged. "Maybe they took a job overseas or something and are going to be gone for months."

"Wouldn't they have taken their kids with them?" Grace asked.

"Not necessarily," Chris responded as he stepped on the milk carton to crush it. "Some parts of the near East, for example, aren't all that safe, but the money's probably too good to pass up. I mean, the real father could be an engineer or something who works in oil. Heck, for all we know the *mom* could be an industrial or chemical engineer."

Aubrey's eyes widened. "Wow. That's what I'll be. A engineer. I want to make lots of money, too, just like Karen's mom."

Johanna laughed. "Chris was just guessing, honey. For all we know Karen and Robby's dad could be an elephant hunter and their mom a hula dancer."

"For real?"

She laughed again. "I'm teasing, although I guess they could be. We'll never know unless Karen or Robby tells us. I'm just surprised they didn't send the kids to boarding school or something. It must be hard on their uncle to suddenly have four young kids living with him, but who knows, maybe the family is close and he's used to it."

The three youngest lost interest after that and fell into a discussion on whether Alexander Snyder was the dorkiest kid in school or not.

"He reads the encyclopedia at the bus stop."

"Yeah, he's up to *F* already."

"*F* for fathead," Stephen giggled.

"Why does he do that?" Johanna wondered. Any kind of intellectual display in front of preadolescents or adolescents, either one, was asking for trouble. "Did you ask him?"

"He says he hungers for knowledge," Will snorted. "Ty told him he was a dorkhead and beat him up after that," he reported matter-of-factly.

"You three better not be part of that," Charlie said on his way through the room, giving Johanna much hope for his future. "You know what Johanna and Mom say all the time."

"You don't have to marry them, but you do have to be kind," they all chorused together.

"That's right," Charlie nodded. "And you better not forget it or when I'm in charge after Jo leaves there may be serious rear end damage done around here. You think she's tough, wait'll you get a load of me."

"Jo won't let you spank us," Aubrey said in her best *nah-nah-nah* voice.

"Jo won't be here."

Before things escalated out of control, Johanna got the four youngest up the stairs and into the bathroom to brush teeth and prepare for bed. She made a mental note to talk to Charlie some time before she moved out about not letting authority go to his head, and prepared for bed herself. She and her mother shared a bedroom. Cognizant of both their needs for privacy, they had put back-to-back shelving units partway down the center of the room. It was an imperfect solution, but provided more storage in a house crammed full of people and their paraphernalia and it gave Johanna the illusion of a space of her own.

Johanna put her bedside light on and climbed into the twin-size bed. Propping up the pillows against the wall behind her bed and settling back against them, she picked up the psychology book she'd been reading from her nightstand and found her place.

Twenty minutes later she snapped it shut, unable to concentrate. Her insides practically bubbled with impatience.

"A few more weeks," she whispered to herself, and got out of bed. Johanna roamed the hall, checking under the doors for patches of light. Charlie and Chris were still up, naturally, and probably would be for a while. Charlie was almost eighteen, so his sleep patterns were his problem, and she was trying to lighten up on sixteen-year-old Chris as well. She wouldn't say anything just yet.

The strip under Stephen and Will's door was dark, but light shone out from under the girls' door. Johanna opened it quietly and peeked in. Aubrey lay sprawled on her stomach, a green-stuffed rabbit clutched close, sound asleep. Grace sat up in bed, reading a laminated, numbered paperback.

"Whole class reading that one?" Johanna whispered as she nodded at the book in Grace's hand.

"Yeah. Mr. Woodley says it's a classic, but it really stinks. I mean, who's gonna take the time to knit the names of people you want dead into your socks?"

"I thought it was a scarf."

"Whatever."

"I can't say I ever cared much for Dickens, either. Twenty more minutes, max, then lights out, okay?"

"This is so boring I'll probably be asleep long before then."

Johanna shut the door.

What was the matter with her? Why was she so restless? Okay, she'd finally be out on her own, working a real job, using her hard-won education in a couple of weeks. It's not as though it was happening tomorrow.

So what was the deal?

Johanna slipped down the steps and rechecked the doors and windows.

It was that guy. That uncle guy. He'd thrown her for a loop without so much as an "excuse me." He'd been seriously cute. *Seriously* cute. Her initial response had been to avoid him. Twice before single fathers on the swim team had seen that she related well to kids and thought she'd be the perfect replacement mother figure for their own little darlings.

Been there, done that. She'd been raising her siblings while her mother worked long hours ever since her dad died. Though she wasn't a mother herself, at twenty-five she'd already done the mother thing.

But had she known Uncle Hunter was only their uncle she might not have dived into the pool quite so quickly. All evening long while she'd swum, checked homework, diverted squabbles and tried to read, he'd been there, just out of reach in her thoughts.

He couldn't have been that special. Probably it was because she'd never seen him before and he'd spent an awful lot of his time looking at her. She'd just been uneasy, that was all.

So maybe he'd be back again tomorrow.

Chapter Two

He was.

Johanna watched him out of the corner of her eye as he settled himself on the hard metal bleacher bench. Two little boys, *really* little boys—like around four and maybe two years old—accompanied him this afternoon. Hunter handed them each a small bag, and the twosome immediately began dragging tiny cars and trucks out, vavooming them over the metal bench and flooring, up Hunter's legs and across his wide chest. Hunter never even flinched.

Johanna was impressed.

She directed her eight-year-olds and unders in a stroke drill and observed while trying not to look as if she was observing.

He was just as good-looking as she remembered. Better. Yesterday her perspective had been clouded by the fact that Johanna had thought Robby and Karen belonged to him, which would have put him right off limits in her book. She'd done everything in her power to convince herself he wasn't all that hot. His eyes were not bluer than blue flames, his chest was not wider than wide and the only reason he probably looked tall at first was because he was standing on the bleachers.

She'd mostly failed.

Johanna lined up her crew behind a starting block after they finished their drill. "Okay, we're going to practice starts now. Marcus, you're up first. Take your mark...*hup!* Let's go, Rebecca. Take your mark...*hup!*"

Now that she knew the children were his only temporarily she felt far more comfortable with that funny feeling she got in the pit of her stomach when Hunter was in the immediate vicinity. She could even admire the ease he displayed around his niece and nephews, in a detached sort of way. Karen and Robby waved in his direction frequently. He was always paying attention and responded. The littlest one had crawled up on his shoulders for a better view of the pool. Hunter held his chubby little legs while small fry pulled his thick, dark hair, bounced up and down and crowed at his older siblings.

"Meet coming up in a few days, my friends. Let's try some relay starts. Aubrey, come into the wall full tilt. Kimmie, get on the block and follow her in with your arms. When she touches, you take off like lightning, but make sure Aubrey's actually touched before you leave the block. Okay, Aubrey, jump into the water halfway down the lane and head on in."

Someday when Johanna was ready to settle down, provided that day ever came once she finally achieved her freedom, Johanna would look for a man like Karen and Robby's uncle.

Someone rock steady.

Dependable.

And sexy as hell.

The sexy as hell part was good enough for now.

"Karen, *walk* over and ask your uncle if you and Robby can stay after for just a few minutes, will you, honey? Let's see if we can get you two to do a flip turn. Okay, Robby, you want to try going off the block?"

"It's too high."

"Once you get used to it, it won't seem so bad."

"Why can't I just go off the edge like before?"

"You can. It's just easier to hold on to the edge of the starting block and you get a better start that way, go out farther right at the very beginning."

"I'm scared."

"Coach Jo, Uncle Hunter says okay, but it's gotta be quick 'cuz the natives are getting restless and he's all out of Cheerios."

Johanna understood the cryptic message perfectly, having used the same cereal many times herself during church services, choir and band concerts and assorted other programs requiring attendance by the care providers of small children.

She acknowledged receipt of his acceptance with a wave to the stands.

Hunter waved back and Johanna's heart flipped. Stupid, but no longer alarming. Without a care in the world, Johanna asked Robby, "How about if I hold your hand?"

Robby thought about it. Hard. "Okay," he finally reluctantly decided. "But you're not gonna let go or anything, are you?"

"Promise." Johanna made a crisscross motion over her heart and extended her hand. "Ready?"

Robby took her hand with all the enthusiasm of a French nobleman ascending the steps to the guillotine. Slowly he climbed the two steps to the top of the block and stood there, well to the rear of the small platform.

"So," Johanna said, "how's the view?"

"Okay," Robby allowed.

"Good. Come on down."

"I don't hafta dive in?" Robby questioned suspiciously, sure he was missing a trick somewhere.

"Not unless you want to."

"I don't."

"Then climb down. That's enough for your first try."

"Karen will think I'm a baby."

"Who cares? She's living in a glass house and I don't think you're a baby. I think you're very brave for getting up there at all."

The youngsters who'd been packing up paused in their tasks and one by one came to stand by the edge as they became aware of the drama being enacted.

In the stands Hunter rose and edged closer after instructing Aaron and Mikie to stay put. "Aaron, don't let Mikie move. I'll be right back."

Karen was getting jealous of the attention Robby was getting. "Get down, Robby," she directed. "I want to try it."

"No. You had a turn before and you wouldn't do it. It's my turn now."

Karen began to whine. "But I wanna try now. You had long enough. It should be my turn again."

It was all Johanna could do not to roll her eyes and ask if Karen wanted a little cheese with her whine. Had it been one of her own siblings, she probably would have, but as it was, she kept her mouth shut and focused on Robby, waiting to see what he would do. Instead, Hunter handled it.

Quietly, so as not to distract Robby, he gently pulled Karen back from the starting block and whispered for her to keep an eye on Aaron and Mikie.

"I don't want you to hold my hand no more. You can let go."

The child's knees were knocking together. "You don't have to, Robbie."

"No, it's okay. Let go."

Johanna did so, but stayed close, ready to step in if Robby lost his newfound courage.

Robbie took a deep breath and straightened his thin shoulders. He stood there, maybe two feet up over the water, looking very much as if he were about to attempt walking a plank.

Hunter took Karen's place, eyes intent on his nephew.

"I'm gonna do it," Robby announced.

"You don't have to," Johanna said. "I just wanted you to see what it was like this first time."

"I'm gonna," he insisted.

"Do you want me to get in the pool and catch you?"

Robby thought about that but evidently decided that, too, would make him a wimp in his sister's eyes. He shook his head. "No," he said.

"All right. If you change your mind I'm right here."

Robby stood there, staring down into the three feet of clear water. Johanna was sure it might as well be a hundred feet deep and shark-infested. Aubrey took her hand on one side, needing the comfort an adult could provide as she remembered her own terror the first few times off the block. "Do you think he's gonna really do it, Johanna?" she whispered.

"Shh," Johanna hushed. "Let him concentrate." She reached out to take Karen's hand with her free hand in a silent signal to remain quiet. What she found was a hand quite a bit larger and hairier than she anticipated. The hand squeezed hers in silent communication, and Johanna about jumped out of her skin. She squealed. Robby startled, lost his balance, windmilled, then fell into the water. He came up sputtering.

"That was fun. Can I do it again?"

"My turn!" claimed Karen.

Hunter whirled around. "Where are Aaron and Mikie?" he asked, his heart suddenly in his mouth.

"Aaron's showing Mikie the other pool. I wanted to watch Robby."

The other pool? *The diving well?* Johanna took off at a

run, Hunter, who'd been frantically sweeping the area with his eyes, in hot pursuit. "Oh, my God," he said. "Oh, my God."

Johanna could see the two little ones leaning over the edge, marveling over, what, the depth of the water? The design on the bottom? Who knew? The swimmers in the other lanes were so involved in their workouts no one else had noticed the tykes, either. Hunter broke into a sprint, passing Johanna as she detoured by the lifeguard stand and grabbed a rescue tube. Hunter had almost reached the pair when Aaron, the four-year-old, slipped on the wet tile and went in, taking little Mikie with him.

"Damn," he said, and dived in, shoes and all. He overshot the pair, who'd already begun to sink and had to turn around, flailing a bit as he trod water and furiously swiped chlorinated water out of his eyes. "Aaron! Mikie!" There! He dived down, but missed and had to come up for air.

Johanna, meanwhile, took the time to kick off her shoes so she wouldn't be so weighted down, tucked the rescue tube under her arms and used a stride entry. Bedlam was rapidly breaking out with shrieking seven- and eight-year-olds alerting the rest of the coaches to the problem. She positioned herself over the children and, holding the tube by its long strap, let her hands come down to her sides, then raised them rapidly up over her head and torpedoed straight down. Coming up behind Aaron, she slipped an arm around him and kicked hard, propelling herself to the surface. She handed him off to Hunter, took a deep breath and went back down.

The smaller one, Mikie, was already limp. Johanna brought him up, then, on her back, pulled him over to the side. The coach of the nine- and ten-year-old group leaned over the side and took the child from her. Johanna put her hands on the pool's edge and lifted herself out.

No need to check the older one. He wailed loudly and hiccuped while squeezing Hunter's neck and being squeezed in return. In true parental fashion, Hunter alternately comforted and berated. "It's okay, you're all right. You ever do anything like that again, I'll drown you myself. Are you sure you're all right? When I tell you to stay put, you need to stay put, hear me? It's okay, calm down. You're strangling me. I've got to check Mikie. Oh, God, something's wrong with Mikie."

Mikie had swallowed a major portion of the pool, Johanna suspected. The other coach had him flat on his back on the pool deck by the time Johanna had lifted herself out of the water. Together they tipped his head back to open his airway. Johanna put her face down close to the toddler's and listened hard while she watched his chest.

"Anything?" the other coach asked.

She shook her head. "I don't think he's breathing."

There was a communal sharp intake of breath.

"Not so close, people," the other coach exhorted. "Give us some room here."

Hunter pushed his way in and knelt by Mikie's head, wanting to do something but feeling helpless. His eyes followed Johanna's every move as she pinched Mikie's little nose and breathed gently into him twice. Hunter watched her face while she searched the side of Mikie's neck with two fingertips.

"He's got a pulse," she announced, and everyone simultaneously sighed. "Call an ambulance, though. He's not breathing." Johanna pinched Mikie's nose and took a breath. Just as she was prepared to deliver it, Mikie began to gag. Moving quickly, she rolled him onto his side, where he proceeded to upchuck what appeared to be a major portion of the water from the diving well all over her, and began to cry. Johanna propped him there on his side so he wouldn't choke, then sat back and closed her eyes.

Hunter scooped up his nephew and held him tightly against his chest. The pressure of the hard squeeze had Mikie upchucking once more, this time down Hunter's back, but Hunter didn't care, he just didn't care. His in-experience and ineptitude hadn't killed anyone. That was what counted.

"Thank you, God," he prayed.

"Amen," whispered Johanna.

Hunter stood up, dripping water, shoes squishing. He had Mikie in his arms and Aaron very quickly attached himself to one leg like a little leech. Karen claimed the other leg and Robby grabbed him from behind. He stood there like an oak and let his heart settle back down into his chest.

"Thank you," he told Johanna gravely, very impressed with the way she'd handled the crisis. She was not just good with children, she was also an incredibly competent woman. Also sexy. Let's not forget the sexy. He became more determined than ever to get to know her.

"You're welcome," she said every bit as gravely.

The coach of the eleven- and twelve-year-olds began to usher people away. "All right, everybody, excitement's over. Let's go finish up. I think tomorrow it might be a good idea if we did some pool safety stuff."

Johanna rose, patted Mikie on the back and turned to leave.

"Wait," Hunter said, grabbing her arm. There was no way he could follow her with the little limpets still attached. "I, uh, wanted to thank you one more time."

"I'm glad we were in time," Johanna returned. Looking into his eyes, she was struck again by just how handsome he was. She shivered and didn't know if it was the sodden clothing dripping down her legs or the sight of gorgeous Hunter covered in children. She took off her shirt and shorts while she thought about that and wrung them out.

Hunter's blood pressure skyrocketed as the woman un-selfconsciously stripped. Damn, but he'd forgotten she wore a bathing suit under her clothes. These sudden adren-aline rushes couldn't be good for a man. He was going to be dead long before his time at this rate.

"I'm sorry this happened. It won't again. I'm still getting used to them."

Johanna nodded. The crisis was over. She was suddenly exhausted. She also wished he'd touch her arm again. There'd been a connection then, almost like a circuit being completed. Maybe his electric blue eyes really were electric. Weird. But Johanna definitely wanted to feel that tingle again. "They move fast, don't they?"

He nodded. "You can say that again. I'm beginning to think they're also at their creative best when they're thinking up new ways to do themselves in."

Johanna laughed weakly. "Yeah. I could tell you some stories about my brothers and sisters that would turn your hair gray just listening."

"I'd like to hear them," he said quietly, and looked directly into her wide eyes. Now he was in danger of drowning in them.

Johanna swallowed. Hard. Oh, God. He wanted to hear her stories. Suddenly she couldn't think of one.

"I'd also like to thank you properly, take you out for dinner or something, but I'm afraid it's too soon to leave the unholy crew with a sitter just yet. They need to settle in a bit and feel more secure." Did they ever. The kids still had nightmares sometimes. Hunter had yet to truly grieve his brother's loss himself. He'd been too busy making it through one day at a time.

"I understand," Johanna said. And she did. Understanding didn't prevent a feeling of disappointment, however.

Someone who liked kids as well as the young swim coach obviously did surely wouldn't mind their being underfoot, so Hunter plowed on. "I can see you're ready for your own workout," he said with a nod at her swimsuit. "But I could stop off somewhere on the way home, get some stuff for ice cream sundaes. I could give you the address—it's not too far—and you could come by the house when you're through."

"Oh, I don't—"

She was going to refuse and Hunter didn't want that. In fact, he wouldn't accept that. "Karen and your Aubrey seem to be hitting it off together. After swimming as hard as they did Aubrey could probably use a sugar infusion. I bet she'd like to come along." He said it just loud enough for the little girl to hear. He hadn't been raising children long, but he'd already learned the unbelievable pressure the little sweethearts could bring to bear when they wanted something. And what little kid wouldn't want ice cream?

Aubrey did not disappoint him.

"Oh, please, Johanna. Can we please go, huh? Can we? Please?" Aubrey folded her hands together in front of her in a supplicating, prayerlike fashion and looked up at her older sister pleadingly. "Will and Steve didn't even have to swim tonight 'cuz Chris got those tickets to the Silver Hawks game at Covaleski Stadium. They're probably having tons of fun. They get to do everything and I hardly ever get to do nothing. Please?"

Johanna rolled her eyes. It was a standard line that every one of her siblings used. Each and every one of them was surely the most abused child in the history of the world. "I hardly ever get to do *anything*," Johanna corrected her. "If you're going to whine, at least do it correctly."

"I hardly ever get to do anything," Aubrey repeated dutifully. "Please?"

She shouldn't let her get away with it, but the truth was Johanna wanted to go herself.

"It's a school night," she said, feeling duty-bound to point out.

"I didn't have any homework." Aubrey quickly inserted the reply, sensing Johanna's wavering as only a child can. "And you made me practice piano before we came. And ice cream's pretty good for you. We made it at school one time. It has milk in it. I saw."

Johanna had to grin. What a little con artist. "Along with

an equal amount of sugar, but what the heck, it's been a traumatic day. We could all use a little comfort food.''

"Yes," chorused Aubrey and Karen together. Karen pumped her fist in the air.

"When Charlie gets here, tell him to take Grace home and check homework for me," Johanna directed her sister. "You can just wait for me to finish up here."

The two girls saluted and raced off with Robby in hot pursuit.

Hunter stood there holding a now quietly sobbing, hiccuping Mikie, and feeling as if Aaron was a permanent attachment. It wouldn't be much longer before he'd forget what life was like with free use of both legs. The three of them dripped water onto the concrete pool deck. His hair was hanging in his face and water rivulets ran down his neck in a decidedly uncomfortable fashion. It was not a setup he would have chosen for asking a woman on a first date. Unfortunately, he had a feeling of foreboding that this was about as good as it was going to get. Probably for years to come. Hunter gave Johanna clear, concise directions and squished his way out of the pool area, lugging Aaron with every step he took.

So much for Mr. Suave Sophisticate.

He sighed. How the mighty were fallen.

He took the two small boys into the boys' locker room, shifted the nozzle on the hand dryer to point down, punched the button and stood them underneath the blast of hot air in a fruitless attempt to dry them out a bit.

Hunter borrowed some towels from the lost and found to spread along the leather seats of his pride and joy. He still cringed as he buckled in those sodden little bodies. His own soggy self wasn't doing the car's seats much good, either. He thought of Johanna's sleek, wet body when she'd stepped out of her shorts and shirt. Now, a body like that, he'd let ruin his leather any day of the week.

"Come on, kids, let's get a move on here," Hunter said,

suddenly in a hurry. How had they left the kitchen? Were there dirty dishes in the sink? Damn, he couldn't remember. He needed to shower, put some dry clothes on. Hunter felt his chin. Maybe he should shave. His five o'clock shadow tended to be heavy.

He stopped at the grocery store on the way home and froze in his damp clothes while he picked up the ice cream and various assorted toppings. He probably went overboard a bit on the topping part, but what the heck, he wanted to make a good impression. Johanna needed comfort food, he'd see she got it. Anything that would buy him time with her.

"That'll be $34.28. Having a party, huh?"

Hunter came to with a start and looked down the checkout counter. He'd spent thirty-five dollars on dessert? Good grief. Well, it would be worth it in the long run. He hoped. "Here you are." He handed over two twenties and waited for his change.

"$5.72. There you go. Have a good night. Enjoy your ice cream, kids."

Aaron and Mikie smiled shyly. Robby grinned and nodded. Karen was the only one who actually got a thank-you out. He was going to have to work on their manners.

Still, they were cute kids, as far as children went, and Johanna was obviously crazy about kids. Thoughtfully, Hunter buckled bodies in and stowed the ice cream in the trunk of the car. "Anybody who takes their safety belt off before this car is in the garage with the engine off, dies. Hear me, Aaron?"

"I won't do it again, I pwomise."

"And no unbuckling anybody else to get them into trouble."

"Okay."

"I mean it."

Hunter watched Aaron nod solemnly in his rearview mirror before grunting and cranking the engine. Maybe he had

Aaron sufficiently cowed. Maybe. In the short time he'd had the children he'd learned it was a mistake to think in absolutes.

"All right, here we go. Keep it down to a dull roar, okay? Uncle Hunter needs to pay attention to his driving. I really don't feel like wrapping us around a pole on the way home."

Hunter strategized as he drove down the quiet streets. He was good at reading people, figuring out what made them tick. It was why he was good at his job. If you wanted to sell major manufacturing systems, you learned how to do that in a big hurry. An effective businessman made small talk with people who liked to chat. He took sports fanatics to the stadium in Chicago or the Hoosier Dome in Indy. Clients who were more into the arts got museum tickets, symphony concert tickets, architectural tours of the city. Whatever it took.

So, what did he know about Johanna and what would his best approach be?

She liked kids. Had to, or she wouldn't surround herself with them. In the world BK—before kids—Hunter would have run as hard and as fast as possible to get away from such a woman, no matter how good-looking she was, but Hunter had entered an alternate world and he was not running away, no indeed.

At any rate, the obvious thing to do here to keep Johanna interested was to surround her with his children. Hunter would make sure they were clean and threaten them with their lives so they'd behave. Hunter nodded thoughtfully. It should work. He nodded more forcefully as he pulled into the garage. His kids were as good—no, better—than any others he'd seen to date. Of course that wasn't saying much in his book, but women thought differently. To his way of thinking, Johanna was a goner.

"Kiss the competition goodbye," he told himself as he pulled into his garage. "You've done it again, Hunter old boy. The woman won't know what hit her."

Chapter Three

Johanna enjoyed her time with Hunter and the children. Heck, she'd grown up with the give-and-take of a large family. Teasing Hunter's niece and nephews was especially fun because she carried no responsibility for them. At the end of the evening she'd be going home, leaving Hunter with the nitty-gritty, day-to-day bedtime-ritual stuff, as well as the long-term physical and personal development stuff. Well, at any rate he was responsible for the long-term development stuff for the short term. How long would the children's parents be gone, anyhow? Hunter seemed to be going to a lot of trouble for a brief period.

Karen had shown her the paint color she'd picked out for her bedroom, a too-sweet cotton-candy pink. Johanna's hands felt sticky just looking at it. She lavished praise. After all, *she* wasn't stuck painting the walls that nauseating color.

Mikie had proudly displayed his new junior bed. He was a big boy now. Johanna was suitably impressed and politely watched as he drove his toy trucks down the wrong side of the road on the track-imprinted play carpet Hunter had installed in Mikie and Aaron's room. After the second pileup, Johanna heartily hoped Mikie did not plan on long distance driving as a viable career choice. Then again, what did it matter? *Johanna* wasn't the one who'd have to teach him right from left, the physics of impact with a large object or see him through to a driver's license later on.

"I went off the starting block and you didn't. That makes you a chicken heart."

"Does not."

"Does, too."

"You only went in 'cuz you fell when Coach Jo yelled."

"Uh-uh."

You know, kids' squabbles were a whole lot funnier when the kids belonged to somebody else. Johanna was having difficulty smothering a smirk as she listened to the byplay.

"Uh-huh," Karen shot back, then turned on Johanna. "Coach Jo, how come you yelled like that? Did you see a spider or something? I hate spiders."

"Karen yells real loud when she sees one, especially if it gets in bed with her."

The mere thought made Johanna shiver, and she had to wonder how the spider got into Karen's bed. After all, she had brothers herself, a fact that made her naturally suspicious.

"Do not."

"Do, too."

Johanna cleared her throat and glanced at her wristwatch. "Just look at the time," she exclaimed. "Why, it's almost eight-thirty! I need to get home or I'm going to miss my bedtime."

Aaron studied her in wide-eyed amazement. "But Miss Johanna, eight-thirty is *our* bedtime, Mikie's and mine. Even Karen and Robby gets to stay up until nine o'clock and you're lots older than them."

"Nine o'clock? Wow. Karen and Robby are lucky ducks,

huh?'' She sighed. ''Poor me. If I'm not in bed on time
I'll be in lots of trouble. Gotta go, guys. Come give me a
hug, then I'm out of here.''

The four of them crowded forward, squeezing and hug-
ging as though starved for affection. Johanna wondered
about their parents again. Her own mother had no choice
but to be gone much of the time. Relatively older at the
time, Johanna had still hated her absence. How could these
little ones possibly understand their parents' desertion?
Wherever they'd taken themselves off to, she certainly
hoped it was worth the separation anxiety their children
were suffering.

And not just the children were suffering.

Hunter looked tired, Johanna thought as she glanced his
way for the thousandth time that night. Darn, but he was
prime male material. The least she could do was get the
kids started in the right direction, she supposed. He looked
as if he could use the help and she didn't mind lending a
hand—as long as she could still go home to her own life
at the end of the day.

Giving the closest two a nudge, she started them on their
way. ''Let's see who can brush their teeth till they shine
the most, okay? Uncle Hunter can be the judge, and you
can make a chart and draw a star by your name if you're
the winner. I bet Uncle Hunter would get a little prize for
whoever has the most stars at the end of the week.''

The kids took off like a stampeding herd.

''I'll be first done.''

''Nuh-uh. I'm gonna beat you.''

Johanna called after them. ''First doesn't count, Robbie,
unless it's also the best.''

''Karen already gots a cabity. So she shouldn't win no
way.''

''You're so stupid'' came the immediate protest. ''It's
just a baby tooth, which is all you've got, big baby. The
dentist said my grown-up teeth would come in like brand-

new and I could start all over again with everything perfect.''

Hunter shook his head as the voices faded up the stairs. ''They're unbelievable, aren't they? I swear they'd argue over whether the sun was going to come up in the morning.'' But he was encouraged by the smile on Johanna's face. It proved he was on the right track. The woman actually liked young children and all the squabbling and immature behavior they entailed. Sick, but who was he to complain? He took her hand. ''I'll walk you to your car.''

Johanna looked down at the big hand swallowing hers. It was large, but Hunter was definitely not ham-handed. He was simply big-boned with long, almost elegantly tapered fingers. His nails were cut blunt, short and were impeccably clean. The back of his hand was lightly furred with glossy deep brown hair.

Johanna stared at those few hairs and couldn't help but wonder about his chest.

Was it hairy or smooth?

She'd bet on hair.

Sparse or plentiful?

A thick, dark mat of hair, she hoped. Thick enough and just coarse enough to make a woman crazy when she pressed up against—what? *What?* She was quite probably the only twenty-four-year-old virgin in town, heck, in the state of Indiana, and here she was daydreaming about *what?*

Good grief.

Johanna ran a hand through her hair, pushing it back off her forehead as she blew out a breath. *Get a grip, Johanna. Before you blow a gasket.*

''Aubrey, sweetheart, run upstairs and tell everybody good-night,'' Johanna instructed, and hoped like heck Hunter wouldn't notice the slight breathlessness in her voice. What was wrong with her? ''I'll wait for you out by the car.''

"Okay," Aubrey agreed, and took off, flying up the stairs. "Be right down. Hey, you guys!"

Shaking his head, Hunter gently tugged on Johanna's hand. He'd meant to merely initiate a little forward propulsion, get Johanna out of the house before his niece's and nephews' behavior degenerated from squabbling into true bickering. Over all, he was pleased with the evening. The kids had generally held themselves together pretty well, if you discounted the near drowning. Judging by Johanna's smiles and easy behavior with them, they'd been a hit, too. However, their behavior was showing definite signs of fraying around the edges. No point in pressing his luck. He wanted her on her way before it became too much of a good thing.

The gentle tug on her hand, however, catapulted Johanna forward. She crashed into his side.

"Oops," Johanna said.

"I'm so sorry," Hunter immediately apologized. "I never meant to pull that hard. Are you all right?" He evidently didn't know his own strength. Leaving the woman black and blue was not the note on which he wanted to end the evening, although he certainly had no argument with having Johanna tucked up against his side. Man, she was warm. And she smelled like ripe fruit. Just the right height for him, too. The top of her head matched the top of his shoulder.

Hunter wrapped an arm around Johanna's waist. He sneaked another sniff of her light perfume when he bent his head to solicitously offer, "Here, let me help you."

Johanna's face burned. Heck, her whole body turned pink. Thank God he couldn't see that. Here the poor man was apologizing all over the place, and the truth was, he hadn't pulled all that hard. She'd only tumbled into him because she hadn't been paying attention. No, Johanna had been lost in a sexual fantasy involving both their naked chests. She could hardly explain that to him, now could she?

So what could she say?

Hunter took a slow step forward, cautiously guiding her, and Johanna immediately stumbled.

Johanna was completely mortified. All her life she'd been an athlete and taken her coordination for granted. Now here she was reduced to tripping over her own feet by a chest she'd never even laid eyes on. It was humiliating, that's what it was. Mortifying and humiliating.

"You okay, honey?"

Ooh, he'd called her honey. Wasn't that the sweetest thing?

"I'm fine. Really. Just a little dizzy spell, I guess. It's already gone. Seriously." Johanna concentrated on her feet until she got outside. For as long as she could remember, she had spent every free moment in or around a swimming pool. She'd done age-group competitive swimming since she'd been seven years old. In that time she'd seen hundreds, no thousands of not just naked male chests, but mostly naked guys. Male racing suits did not leave a whole lot to the imagination.

In all that time never had she reacted like this.

Left foot. Okay, now your right foot. Almost there.

When Johanna got home she'd have her mother feel her forehead. Maybe she was getting sick and didn't even know it yet.

It was possible.

They reached her vehicle without further mishap. Johanna breathed a prayer of thanksgiving.

Thank you, God.

Hunter propped an elbow against her minivan's roof. "So, I guess the crew and I will be seeing you again tomorrow." With the nonsupporting hand he tucked a lock of hair back behind her ear.

As his hand skimmed the side of her face briefly, Johanna's skin tingled. She stared at him uncomprehendingly. "Wha—oh, right. You mean swim practice." She nodded her head. "Yes. I'll be there. Absolutely." *Oh, for crying out loud. Get a grip, girl.*

"I know I've already told you... I wish I knew what else I could do other than repeat myself over and over. Thanks again for everything you did earlier. Here, too. I like the chart and star idea. Sure cut down on arguments over getting ready for bed. And I know I'll be watching Aaron and Mikie a lot closer from now on."

"It's okay," Johanna murmured. Oh, she was in a sad way. Just watching his lips move had her mesmerized. She was having trouble attaching meaning to the words and probably sounded as if she'd left her IQ at home. She looked away from his mouth and cleared her throat. "Seriously. It's okay. Part of the job description. Although maybe we, uh, that is to say, you ought to think about getting the little ones some swimming lessons. You know, at least get them to the point where they can tread water so somebody at least will have enough time to get to them next time they go in the drink."

Hunter stared into those brown doe eyes. "Absolutely. It's already on my list. I'll see to it." He straightened away from the car and leaned forward to brush her forehead with his lips. "I'll see you then. Tomorrow."

Johanna nodded solemnly. Tomorrow. Then she took a deep breath and put a hand over her heart. Man alive, the poor little thing was working overtime for sure. Her entire chest wall was heaving. You'd have thought he'd just asked her to help practice some of the more difficult positions from the *Kama Sutra*. Not that she'd ever seen a copy, but Johanna had an extremely vivid imagination and her heart wasn't the only thing working overtime just then. No, it wasn't.

A mower whined somewhere down the block. Across the street the dog that never shut up barked away. Children's voices drifted down from an open window on his own second story. In short, the neighborhood was alive with sound. But Hunter's gaze drifted from her wide brown eyes down to her mouth. He became so focused on her barely parted lips and slightly crooked front tooth that the surrounding cacophony became nothing more than a background white noise. Once more he leaned forward.

She didn't need a road sign to know what came next.

Johanna's breath caught in her throat. And there went her heart again.

She didn't kiss on a first date and this could hardly even be called that. Some guy buying you ice cream out of gratitude for saving his kid's life wasn't a date, now was it? Especially since there'd been five kids in clear view the entire time. Speaking of which, Aubrey might come out at any minute. She'd be shocked. For sure she'd blab.

Johanna was an expert at blocking this kind of move on a guy's part. A step back, a lowered head, even a quick insertion of some bright conversational gambit. All worked.

But then, maybe she was reading too much into this kiss. It could be.

Wasn't it possible that Hunter was simply a toucher? You know, not touchy feely in a bad kind of way, just…tactile. This could be nothing more than a sort of nonverbal appeal to a different one of the senses kind of thing. He'd done the verbal thing and was moving on. Could well be she'd get a thank-you card in the mail sometime soon. Who knew? Maybe he kissed everybody goodbye. For all she knew, he might have some French blood in his heritage. Then it wouldn't be a first date kind of kiss, but just a social kind of thing. The French were always kissing one another.

Johanna angled her head to better meet Hunter's kiss. She'd never been kissed by a Frenchman.

Their lips met and Johanna had to reach for the car door

handle to steady herself. Holy smoke. He'd barely touched her with his lips and she was already reeling.

"Hell," Hunter muttered, and moved closer, crowding her just a bit, but not enough that she could really lodge a legal protest.

He skimmed the back of his knuckles down her cheek, which gave her the shivers. He noticed and did it again. Then Hunter slid the backs of those same knuckles down the side of her chest, barely catching the beginning curve of her breast. Again, not quite enough to warrant a complaint but more than enough to have her questioning what she'd thought was a well-conditioned heart. He let his hand rest on her waist.

Oh, boy, here it came.

Once more their lips met. Not quite as brief, not quite as sweet and innocent.

Carnal was a good descriptive word that came to mind.

His tongue slid slowly along the seam of her closed mouth.

She could take a hint when she was hit over the head with one and Johanna parted her lips.

"That's it," he muttered, and tugged carefully on her bottom lip with his teeth.

The screen door slapped. Johanna and Hunter both startled.

Johanna pushed on his shoulders. It was like trying to move stone. Unable to see over his shoulder she had to lean and look around it. "Aubrey! Uh, hi! You ready to go?"

"All set." The child paused on her way down the front steps, studying the two of them curiously. "What are you two doing?"

Johanna colored guiltily. "Nothing. Just saying goodnight. That's all."

"Yeah, uh-huh."

Damn, but for seven she had a suspicious mind.

"Were you guys *kissing?*"

Johanna shoved once more. This time he released her. "No. Absolutely not."

Hunter swung around. "Yes."

"I *knew* it!" Aubrey crowed. "That is so *gross!*"

Hunter began an exaggerated stalk. "I kiss all the beautiful women that cross my path." He stopped and pointed like a well-trained setter. "What's this? Another beautiful woman?"

"To be," Johanna inserted.

"Another beautiful woman to be?" Hunter repeated dutifully.

"Oh, no, not me. Johanna, make him stop," Aubrey ordered as she giggled and danced away. "You're not doing that to me."

"Oh, I think so," Hunter insisted, still stalking as the seven-year-old backed up with both hands held in front of her in a weak attempt to ward him off. "Do you know what happens to little girls who think my kissing is gross?" he asked menacingly.

Aubrey was laughing so hard she could barely get the words out. "No, what?"

He lunged and caught her.

She shrieked.

Hunter questioned his wriggling burden one more time. "So you don't think you'd like my kisses, hmm?"

Aubrey shook her head emphatically.

"I'll give you ten years, my little pullet," Hunter said. "Then we'll see what you have to say about the subject."

She really shrieked then and folded up laughing as he gently tickled her.

"I still think it's gross and I'm still gonna tell," Aubrey managed to say between giggles. "I'm gonna tell everybody you and Johanna were kissing."

Just as Hunter was preparing a reply, a young voice yelled down from up above. "Uncle Hunter? Mikie threw

Aaron's toothbrush in the potty while I was using it. Then he flushed it down all because Aaron said his teeth were whiter than Mikie's and Mikie probably wouldn't get no stars. How's Aaron gonna brush his teeth now? We coulda cleaned it up, couldn't we? I mean, if we used lots and lots of soap? But it's gone now. Mikie flushed it down. Aaron's really mad 'cuz he only got half his teeth done. I think maybe it was the top half, but it coulda been the bottom. Want me to ask him?''

"No, just hang on. I'll be there in a minute," Hunter called up. "I'm taking care of important business down here right now."

"Hunter," Johanna broke in anxiously. "Did you hear what he said? Mikie threw Aaron's toothbrush down the toilet. It's going to overflow."

"Yeah, yeah. I'm getting used to it. You forget. I've already had the little monsters for over a month. It took me that long to get things taken care of at my brother's place." Hunter kept his attention focused on Aubrey. "So what do you say, pip-squeak? You still planning on telling? Is it worth another ice cream sundae not to?"

"I gotta tell. I heard Charlie telling Chris he didn't think Johanna had ever kissed anybody at all. He said she was a freak of nature. So see? I gotta tell them Johanna's not ab... ab...''

"Abnormal?"

"Charlie said what?" Johanna gasped indignantly.

"Yeah, what you said. Abnormal."

"You tell Charlie and Chris that Johanna not only knows how to kiss but that I said she's a world champion kisser. Tell them I said I'd rather take on the world heavyweight boxing champion than your sister."

Johanna had edged closer to Hunter and Aubrey, the better to defend herself. In an eye-blurring move, Hunter released Aubrey and steadied her with one hand while snagging Johanna around the waist with his other arm. He then proceeded to bend her backward over his arm and give her a loud smacking kiss. Then he collapsed on the grass to clutch his chest. "Look. See? We're going to have to start calling her Killer. Her kisses are so potent they knocked me right over."

Johanna turned red and prodded him with her foot. "Stop it, you fool. Get up. You're putting on a show for the entire neighborhood." But even the playful kiss had affected her. She took a deep breath to settle her pulse. "I don't believe this. I'm leaving. Aubrey, get in the car. Open your mouth when we get home and die."

Aubrey skipped alongside her sister to the car. "I gotta tell," she insisted. "You said family sticks up for one another even if we can't stand their guts. I gotta tell them you're not ab...ab whatever."

"Don't you worry," Johanna said, stuffing her younger sibling into the automobile. "I fully intend to have a talk with Charles and Christopher both."

"They're in big trouble now," Aubrey whispered out the window to Hunter. "Did you hear? She used their whole names."

"Break both their heads..." Johanna continued to mutter as she turned the key in the ignition. "Crack them open like soft boiled eggs, to which their brains bear a striking resemblance. Couple of idiots, that's what—"

"Uncle Hunter, Robby just—"

"I'm on my way, Karen," Hunter interrupted as he watched the car drive down the street. The moment was lost. He couldn't help but regret it. He hadn't been lying. The woman's kisses were damned potent. "Be right there." With a sigh of resignation and a great sense of desertion, he turned and headed back into the house. How in the world could he feel lonely? He was surrounded by little bodies full-time, nonstop. And yet when he'd watched Johanna's car turn the corner and go out of sight, that's exactly how he felt. All alone.

He'd have to figure it all out later, Hunter supposed. Right now he had a toilet to uproot.

Johanna drove home, her mind in a turmoil. She couldn't help but wonder if her subconscious mind wasn't naturally perverse. Here she was within a month of being free as a breeze for the first time in her life. She'd be done with her schooling and Charlie would take over her role here with the family. Johanna was all set to get her own apartment, have some actual privacy, and she was suddenly being slammed with all these feelings and emotions for some guy? Heck, even if he was, uh, unencumbered, so to speak, Johanna had already decided to enjoy herself for the next several years. Play the field. See what—and who—was out there. But her own body and mind were betraying her. What to do?

She pulled into the garage and put the door down. Aubrey ran ahead.

Johanna was so wrapped up in her own mental musings she forgot to reinforce her previous warnings with another death threat.

"So, I heard you were kissing some guy right out on his front lawn, is that right, big sister?" Charlie greeted her.

"I am going to murder that child," Johanna muttered as she threw her car keys down on the countertop. "Where is she?"

"She ran upstairs to tell Grace and Stevie," Chris reported.

Johanna shut her eyes. She couldn't wait to move out and have a little privacy. Even ten minutes would seem like manna from heaven right now.

"So," Charlie began again. He seemed to begin every other sentence that way, Johanna had noticed. "How was it? Open or closemouthed? Was this guy any good? Come on, give."

With a conscious effort Johanna undid the tightly

clenched fists her hands had become. "I refuse to discuss kissing technique with my little brother."

"Why not?" he asked. "It's not like you're going to corrupt me or anything. I'm seventeen now, a fact you seem to continually forget. All grown up. I've been kissing girls for a long time now. After all, not everyone in this house is socially retarded." Charlie dismissed his hopeless sister with a flick of his finger. "Heck, you probably couldn't rate his technique if you tried. I bet this was your first time, wasn't it?"

"No, it was not," Johanna replied between ground teeth. "Some of us simply understand the meaning of the word *discretion,* that's all. PDAs, as I believe I've mentioned more than once or twice since your girlfriend Molly's started coming around, are in extremely bad taste."

"What's a PDA?" Aubrey asked as she reentered the kitchen.

"Never mind," Johanna instructed.

"Public displays of affection," Charlie informed her.

Aubrey nodded wisely. "Oh, you mean like when Charlie and his friends are in the basement playing pool and you send me down there to make a nuisance of myself. The guys are all wrapped around the girls and they all jump apart whenever I come down. Once Charlie whapped his chin on Molly's head and he started to fall. Somehow his hand got caught on the inside of Molly's shirt so that when he almost fell over Molly's shirt got pulled way out. Molly yelled at him for almost tearing her new shirt, too. It was funny."

"Charlie, I'm going to murder you. In cold blood I'm going to murder you. Keep your hands out of Molly's blouse, you hear me? And if I'd wanted her to know the definition of PDA, I'd have told her myself," Johanna said.

Charlie blew her off in typical brotherly style. "You're the one that brought it up and you're the one who keeps sending the little kids down into the basement. You think

I'm not on to your tricks? Lighten up and quit being so repressed. This is the twenty-first century now. She's seven. She can handle it, can't you, Aub?''

Aubrey nodded seriously. ''Sure, I could if I wanted, but who'd want to? Kissing is so-o disgusting, you know? I mean, unless it's Mom or someone.''

''Keep thinking that way, kid,'' Johanna encouraged. ''I like the way your mind works.''

''Come on, Jo,'' Charlie said, cupping his hands and holding them eight inches out from his chest. ''Even you have to admit Molly is hot.''

''Meaning her boobs are huge.''

''Yeah.''

''What else does she have going for her, Charlie?''

He appeared genuinely puzzled. ''What do you mean?''

Briefly Johanna closed her eyes. ''I mean what's going on up there in her attic? She got a treasure trove up there or a couple of lonely dust motes?''

''Who cares?''

''You should.''

''Why?''

''Why? I'll give you why. Because you've been dating her for a while. You're almost eighteen. By definition that means you're in the middle of hormone hell. Things can escalate out of your control before you even know it.''

''One can only hope,'' Charlie said fervently.

''Don't be stupid,'' Johanna said disgustedly.

''What's stupid?'' he returned indignantly. ''I'm telling you the woman has a body to die for. A man reaches his sexual peak at eighteen. I read that somewhere. Heck, another year and I'll have missed my prime altogether. End up a dried-out prune like you.''

Johanna stared at her brother, who was suddenly a stranger to her. ''Aubrey,'' she directed. ''Go on in the other room and get your practicing done.''

''I already did.''

"Practice some more."

"Why do I have to?"

"Because I said so. Go."

"You're supposed to explain your reasoning to children, Jo. Even I know that," Christopher chipped in.

"Chris, this doesn't concern you, and I used to try and explain the whys of things to you, but you wore me out. 'Why do I have to eat my vegetables?' Because they're good for you. 'Why are they good for you?' Because they have vitamins. 'Why do I need vitamins when we have those chewable ones?' I mean, come on, Chris. Eventually you end up back at eat your vegetables because I said so. I'm just trying to save a little time here, cut to the chase. Now, butt out." Johanna crossed her arms over her chest and stared at her brother. "So, Charlie, you've been discussing the facts of life with Chris, is that right?"

"Yeah," Chris interrupted not at all intimidated by being told to butt out. "Charlie told me all kinds of interesting stuff. Did you know..." And Chris proceeded to reel off a long list of sexual misinformation that left Johanna's jaw dropping and her tongue about falling out of her mouth.

Johanna stared at her two brothers, dumbfounded. "Charlie, I cannot believe what I am hearing. I know I gave both you and Chris a book to read and I know for a fact you had some sex education stuff at school. I had Mom sign the release."

Chris answered very earnestly. "Charlie says no teacher at school is really going to tell the whole truth."

"That's ridiculous. Why would they lie? And what about the book I gave you two? Didn't you bother to read it? I'm quite sure it didn't say anything about these things you mentioned."

"Did you see the copyright on that thing?" Charlie sneered. "It was 1991. Practically the Dark Ages. They probably still hadn't figured things out completely."

Johanna threw up her hands in exasperation. "There are

holes in your logic big enough to drive trucks through, Charlie. You refuse to see them because it would mean having to exercise a little self-control. And it'll have to be you. Molly appears to have no morals to speak of. I don't know why she bothers buttoning her blouse in the morning. I hate to be the one to burst your little bubble, but just in case you've forgotten, let me just remind you that there is no one-hundred-percent-effective birth control method. You'd better find out a little more about this girl than her bra size. Mistakes happen. Is this someone you're willing to share your genetic code with?''

"Take a chill pill, Jo, nothing's going to happen. Condoms are, what, something like ninety-five-percent-effective."

"And if you fall into the other five percent?"

"I won't," he said with all the in-bred confidence of the adolescent.

"Right. Of course not. Silly me. I give up. I'm going to get Mom to talk to you. Maybe you'll listen to her." And Johanna flounced out of the kitchen.

In light of the evening's events, Johanna knew this conversation was getting her in over her head. Just how much did she know about men? And how deeply did she want to get involved with one of the alien species?

Chapter Four

Johanna stormed up the stairs, muttering the whole way. "That boy is in serious testosterone overdrive and Chris isn't all that far behind. Talk about the blind leading the blind—Charlie is the *last* person who should be bringing Chris up to speed on sex." Johanna snorted and caught the banister as she almost tripped. "Stevie! Come get your gym shoes off the steps before somebody kills themselves!" she yelled. Johanna continued to mutter as she marched up.

She reached the door of the bedroom she shared with her mother and swung it open with undue force. "Mother? You in here?"

"Right here, Johanna. You sound a little frazzled, sweetie, what's the matter? Everything seemed under control downstairs when I came up."

"Your son, that's what's the matter. And I do mean what, not who. You're going to have to talk to him, Mother. He's on the fast track to ruin and disaster."

Johanna stopped ranting long enough to get a good look at her mother. Then she glanced down at her sports wristwatch, her brow furled. "You never go to bed this early. It's only nine o'clock. Are you sick?"

"I was just a little tired, that's all. Thought I'd go to bed and read a little bit."

"You haven't got a book," Johanna pointed out. "You're just staring off into space."

"Thinking," her mother assured her. "Just thinking."

"Uh-huh. Thinking. Not happy thoughts judging by the look on your face. Just exactly what are you thinking about?" Johanna moved more fully into the room and shut the door behind her. Leaning back against it, she studied her mother. At forty-three, Madelyn Durbin looked ten years younger. Life hadn't been particularly kind to Maddie, but she'd never let it get her down. Maddie was Johanna's heroine. Johanna's mother, currently a sales rep for a local software firm out of necessity rather than ambition, had always taken life's lemons and done her utmost to produce lemonade. Tonight, the expression on her mother's face said today's batch was in need of more sugar. A lot more sugar. "Problems at work?" Johanna probed. She moved over to her mother's bed and sat on the edge. Placing one hand on her forehead, Johanna said, "You don't feel feverish. Come on, give."

"It's nothing a little time won't take care of," her mother assured her. "I promise. Now, which one of the boys is giving you grief?"

Johanna flopped back across the foot of her mother's bed. "Charlie. He's downstairs acting like he's personally responsible for the discovery of sex. I think he and Molly are active, Mom, you know, sexually active, and he's doing his best to convince Chris that sex should be every teenage boy's goal in life. Someone's got to talk to them, Mom, set them straight."

Maddie sighed. "And that someone needs to be me."

"It's a little bit out of my line, Mom. I don't want to

even think about my little brother's sex life, much less discuss it with him.''

"And you somehow think I want to discuss it with my baby boy?''

Johanna rolled off the bed. "Give it up, Mom. It ain't gonna work. This is above and beyond the call of duty. It's all yours.''

Maddie sighed once more. "I guess. Sometimes parenting just stinks. Especially single parenting. This is when a boy needs his father. And you know what? You just don't think about this kind of thing when you and your husband bring home your little bundles of joy. Babies are so cute. You keep them warm, dry and well fed and they coo and smile and everybody coos and smiles right back at them, they're so adorable. Unfortunately, they're like one of those cute fluffy kittens we saw at the animal shelter. They're so sweet you tend to forget they're going to grow up. Turn into a cat on you. A cat that brings dead mice into the house and stalks the birds out in the yard. By the time you realize that, it's too late. You're hooked. You love them and you're stuck with them.''

"Mom, don't go getting all philosophical on me. Just answer one question for me. Are you ready to be a grandmother?''

Her mother blanched. "Good God. I'm still not sure if I'm ready to be a parent yet.''

Boy, her mother really was in a strange mood. Johanna didn't have time right then to focus on that just then. There was enough on her plate already. She pressed her point.

"And are you ready to raise your grandchild? Because if Charlie gets Molly pregnant that's exactly what's going to happen. They've got too much schooling ahead of them to do it themselves.''

"All right, all right. He needs the facts of life explained to him. Again. But if it didn't sink in the first one hundred times I went through this with him and gave him my expectations, what makes you think it's going to sink in now? At this point in his life he's not going to listen to his mother. What we need is the male perspective.''

Johanna snorted. "We've already got that, Mom, and it's pretty warped. You wouldn't believe some of the stuff he told Christopher.''

Maddie waved her hand. "No, no, not the adolescent male. Somebody mature, but not so old they can't relate, you know? Young enough that Charlie and Chris can look up to him. Cool, you know? Somebody with some style and flash but has his head on straight." Maddie raised her knees under the sheets, leaned forward to hug them with her arms and rested her chin on the tops of her knees while she thought out loud. "There are a couple of guys at work, but they're too old—my age—for Chris and Charlie to really listen to." Maddie rolled her eyes. "Nice guys but they wear pocket protectors in their shirt pockets. Charlie and Chris would eat them alive.''

Then her mother threw the ball into Johanna's court.

"Can you think of anybody, Jo?"

An immediate image of Hunter Pace popped into mind. He was tall, he was broad-shouldered and lean-hipped. In other words, a blue-eyed, dark-haired jock. Adolescent boys respected jocks. Heck, Charlie had three shoe boxes of baseball cards in his closet along with a football signed by last year's Notre Dame quarterback.

Hunter's hair was still a rich dark brown without a speck of gray, its cut stylish without looking styled. He seemed to have a permanent five o'clock shadow that gave him a slightly dangerous look, which ought to appeal to the brain of an adolescent still struggling to nurture any facial hair at all.

He was responsible without flaunting it. He had no children of his own, but look how he was baby-sitting for his brother's children. He'd be perfect for the job of explaining the perils of casual sex to a couple of hormonally driven adolescents who thought with their, um, male organs.

And yet, there was something about the man, something she couldn't put her finger on. Somehow Johanna just knew that Hunter Pace wasn't quite…safe or even totally…tame. Somehow she knew the less she had to do with him, the better.

"No," she stated quite firmly. "I don't know anybody like that."

Maddie stared thoughtfully into space. "The guy can't be someone who has totally sold out to the establishment— no wingtips, but successful. Someone who attracts women but respects them. He can't be a user."

Johanna bit back a disgusted sound. "Try Mount Olympus." Then she shook her head. "Never mind, scratch that. Even the gods were users."

Maddie looked right in her eyes and delivered the coup de grace. "What about that man you and Aubrey went to see tonight? Would he do?"

Johanna shook her head violently. She was not going to ask Hunter Pace to talk sex with her brothers. No way. Absolutely not.

"Whoever talks to them, he's got to be hot, or whatever the current word is," Maddie mused. "You know, a hunka munka. This guy have any obvious physical defects the boys would jump on? Part his hair in the middle? Pull his pants up too high? Aubrey said you let him kiss you, and I know how selective you can be. He's got to be practically perfect."

Johanna flushed beet red. She really was going to strangle that child. "Okay, the guy is hot. His pants aren't falling off his butt like Charlie's but they're not up under his arms, either. And the whole thing was a big nothing, okay? Nothing. His two nephews got away from him at the pool, fell in and I pulled them out. The man was grateful, that's all. He treated Aubrey and me to some ice cream and gave me a peck out of gratitude. End of story.''

Maddie arched a brow. ''Where'd he give you this little peck? Pecks of gratitude are usually on the cheek.''

''So, okay, it was on my mouth, big deal. I swear it was still a little peck of gratitude. He probably just missed or something.'' Who was she kidding? The man hadn't missed. He'd gotten what he'd aimed for and Johanna's pulse picked up just thinking about it.

''Aubrey says he had to help you into the car, that you couldn't stand too well after that little peck of gratitude.''

''Aubrey's going to get her tongue tied back to her tonsils.'' Was there anyone the child hadn't told? The kid would probably take an ad out in the paper if Johanna didn't get a gag on her posthaste.

''Well, we'll have to see who else we can think of,'' her mother said, ''because I really don't think a lecture from me is going to do too much good.''

Johanna could have sworn she heard her mother mutter ''for more reasons than one'' as she swept back out of the room to go bang on the bathroom door and harass whoever was loitering in there to move it. ''Come on, come on!'' she yelled. ''You're not the only one who has to use the bathroom. Unless you're naked, unlock the door. All I want to do is brush my teeth.''

''Be out in a minute'' came the muffled response.

Yeah, right, and if she believed that they probably had a bridge they'd like to sell her.

Why would her mother say something like that, though? What other reasons could there be? She must have misheard. Her mother had seemed distracted. She'd probably been muttering about something else altogether.

Over the next two days Johanna almost convinced herself that she'd overreacted to Hunter's kiss. She got the younger ones off to school in the mornings, made sure they had lunches and then attended her classes at the South Bend branch of Indiana University. Sure, she had some trouble staying focused, but that was probably more due to the dry subject matter. The little hearts she caught herself doodling along with the various calligraphic versions of the name Hunter she'd ornately drawn in the margins meant nothing. Really.

Johanna found herself talking to herself in the student lounge, however.

"He stares at me all during swim practice. How am I supposed to concentrate on the little ones with his eyes boring a whole through my back? Someone could drown and I wouldn't even notice."

"Why doesn't Mom do something about Charlie? God knows I've bugged her enough about it. For that matter, what's wrong with Mom? She's so…out of it or something. I hope she's not getting sick."

Johanna sat up straight in her chair. "God, I hope she's not having problems at work. The paper said a lot of companies are downsizing. What if she loses her job?"

The couple at the next table picked up their trays and moved a distance away.

Johanna nodded her head. "Great. Now I'm getting spooky and scaring people away. Terrific."

"Is this a private conversation or can anyone jump in?"

Johanna glanced up.

"Hunter! What are you doing here?"

"I met a client for lunch. Hired a neighbor on the block who does child care to watch Aaron and Mikie for the day. On my way back to the office I thought I'd run in and pick up one of the community adult education brochures. I was just cutting through the student lounge on my way back to the car and I saw you. How about you? What are you doing here?"

"Me? Going to school." Johanna gestured to the open book and notebook in front of her. "Two more weeks and

I'm finished. An officially educated woman ready to face the challenges of the new millennium.''

"Congratulations.''

Johanna leaned back in her chair. ''It's taken longer than it should have because I had to take over the running of the house when my mom went back to work, but I am this close—'' she held up her hand, forefinger and thumb almost touching ''—to being ready to take on the world.''

"Kind of a daunting thought,'' Hunter said.

"Not for me. Just give me a push in the right direction and I'll be off and running.''

Johanna was feeling safe. She was surrounded by people. Surely she was too inhibited to jump on him in front of a group. ''Do you have time to sit down for a minute? I'm getting a crick in my neck looking up at you.''

"Oh, sorry.'' Hunter pulled out the chair across from Johanna and dropped into it. He set the university's brochure down on the table in front of him.

Johanna smiled at him and nodded in the direction of the brochure. ''So, what are you thinking about taking?''

"There are a couple of parenting classes I thought might be useful. I'm telling you, the two-year-old brain does not function normally. I think it takes several years where the synapses just try various connections up there until something works. Meanwhile, you're just kind of left in the dark not knowing what the heck the kid is going to do next and when he does it it's a total mystery as to why he did.''

"What did Mikie do now?''

Hunter blew out a breath. ''The question should be, what hasn't he done yet? The list would be a lot shorter. That child is a complete enigma. Along with Aaron, Robby and Karen, of course.''

Johanna grinned. ''Ah, it'll all be over before you know it. They'll be gone and you'll wonder where the time went.'' He really was a good man, Johanna thought. Dangerous, but good. She smiled at him. She'd dealt with her share of two- and four-year-olds. Any way you looked at it, they were a whole lot funnier when they belonged to somebody else. In a few short months he'd be laughing about all their ridiculous capers. "Look at it this way," she advised. "It's good practice for when you have kids of your own."

Now he was convinced she was crazed. Johanna had been talking to herself when he'd noticed her sitting there and now she honestly thought he'd purposely add to the mayhem in his life? Hunter leaned forward and spoke slowly, each word distinct. "I am never, I repeat *never* going to have children of my own. Do I look stupid? Do I look *insane?*"

She sat back in her chair, brows arched. Well, that was certainly emphatic enough. Never was a long time. Johanna studied Hunter carefully. That toothbrush must have been a lot harder to get out of the toilet than he'd allowed for. But even if he was having a bad day or a couple of days, "never" was still fairly emphatic…a long time. Certainly time enough for her to flirt a bit, enjoy his company a bit. Hmm.

There was still that nagging sense of danger, though.

Then she thought of her mother. She'd been acting really weird lately. Going to bed really early, sleeping most of the past weekend away. And there was no getting around she still hadn't talked to Charlie and Chris. Johanna didn't think she was going to.

Darned if Johanna was going to do it—like they'd almost listen to her, anyway. And Johanna was not raising any more children, not even her own brother's. Suddenly she felt daring. She leaned forward. "I'll make a deal with you."

Hunter was immediately suspicious. Last time he'd made a deal he'd ended up with four children to raise and he'd had none of the fun of producing them. As far as Hunter was concerned, that was the crowning blow right there.

"What kind of deal?" No more of this "you can name me in your will when you have kids if I can name you in mine now" stuff. He no longer speculated in the futures market.

"You must have a list of things you need to get done. You know, things around the house, errands."

Hunter rolled his eyes. "Only about a mile long."

"Wouldn't it be easier to knock some of those jobs off without the kids underfoot?"

Hunter only grunted. That was too obvious to deserve a real answer.

"How about if I take the kids—all four of them—and keep them Saturday afternoon. That would give you close to six hours to do whatever you want all by yourself." Johanna waggled her eyebrows at him.

It sounded like a damn miracle, only Hunter had given up believing in those. He was, however, still interested enough to at least nibble on the bait a little bit. "Sounds good," he allowed cautiously. Good enough to do almost anything in return, but not being stupid he mentally underscored the "almost." "What do you get in return?"

Johanna sat back and drew a design on the tabletop with her finger. "Oh, nothing much. Did I mention I'd feed them lunch as well?"

She was already sweetening the bait and he'd yet to hear his part of the deal. If anything, he became more leery.

"Before you get out the peanut butter and jelly let's hear the payback. I learned a long time ago there's no such thing as a free lunch. You're dangling a four-course meal in front of a starving man. You must want something pretty badly in return. What is it?"

"Practically nothing," Johanna hastily assured him. "I swear, just an eensy teensy little favor, that's all."

"How eensy?" he demanded suspiciously. "Exactly what does this eensy teensy little favor involve?"

"Ah—" How to explain? This was so impromptu and she was no good at that. Johanna needed time to think and plan. Of course, in this type of situation all the planning in the world probably wouldn't help get her tongue around the words she wanted to get out. She blew out a breath of frustration. "Oh, forget it. Never mind."

Johanna flipped her notebook and book shut, stacked them and started to rise. Hunter grabbed her wrist and tugged her back down. "I didn't say no, I'm just not saying yes until I hear the whole thing. I don't sign blank contracts."

"It would never work, anyway."

"Why don't you let me be the judge of that? If it's at all reasonable, I'll do it. I'd practically kill to have a free Saturday. In fact, I'm no longer sure I'd even stop short of murder. Come on, spill it."

Oh, heck, what did she care what he thought of her?

She cared.

But caring could be overruled by desperation.

Johanna took a deep breath. "Okay, here's the thing. My brother seems to think Don Juan is his middle name."

Hunter held up a hand. He'd met her brother. He'd have thought Shy was his middle name. Or Mr. Mumble-Into-His-Chest. "Will? We're talking about Will here?"

"No, not Will. Charlie."

Hunter made no attempt to hide his confusion. "Who's Charlie? I thought your brother's name was Will. Oh, and I remember there was another one. Stephen, right?"

"There are two more besides them. Charlie's seventeen. He's corrupting Chris, the sixteen-year-old."

"Holy smoke, you've got a big family."

"Tell me about it. I could handle them when they were all little, but like I said, Charlie's seventeen now—"

"What'd they do, split a six-pack? Listen, I did that once in high school, too. Got sick as a dog. Did they get good and sick, I hope? Trust me, they'll never overimbibe again. You get real tired real fast of throwing up your brains."

"I'll have to take your word for that."

Hunter looked at Johanna curiously. "You've never been drunk, have you?"

"No. I skipped over that part of the adolescent ritual, thank you. Now, about Charlie, that's not the problem, although now that you mention it he missed his curfew last Saturday and Sunday morning he said he couldn't go to church because he thought he had the flu." Johanna slapped the tabletop. "Darn it, I never even thought to smell his breath when he came in."

Hunter patted her hand. "It's all right. You can smell it this weekend. If he didn't make himself sick enough to actually throw up, you no doubt still have time to catch him in the act. Let's get back on track here. Drinking's not the problem. What is?"

"Sex," Johanna announced baldly, and was inordinately pleased she'd gotten it out.

It was Hunter's turn to sit back. "Sex? You want me to explain the facts of life to your brother? Isn't he a little old to still believe in the stork?"

"Actually my mother found me under the leaves in a cabbage patch."

"Really? Mine at least got me from the hospital, which is a lot more sanitary than some muddy field."

Johanna drummed her fingers on the table. They were getting off track here. "This is all very interesting, I'm sure, but not the point. Charlie understands the *how* part just fine. In fact, the differences between the male and female plumbing and how the two fit together seems to be the only part of mother's and my discussions he seems to have grasped with any degree of certainty, or at any rate retained."

"You're losing me here, Johanna," Hunter warned.

"Look, the kid understands the mechanics of sex just fine, okay? More than fine. It's just that he seems to be stuck in concrete learning, all right? There's no deductive reasoning going on here. He either can't or won't progress to any sort of comprehension of cause and effect. And it's the effect part I'm worried about.'' She studied him for a moment, a plea in her eyes. "Charlie has filled Chris's head with a lot of sexual mythology. They both need to be straightened out and they aren't going to listen to their big sister.'' Johanna stared at him hopefully. "Will you do it?''

"I get this Saturday afternoon and next Saturday as well.''

"What?''

Hunter shrugged. "Take it or leave it. It's a big job you've set before me. A man—or boy—tends to be stubborn about sex, convincing themselves it's necessary for their mental and physical well-being.'' He grinned at her and her heart flipped in her chest. "At your brothers' age sex is the only constant in their thought stream. It's probably in the forefront of their brain ninety-five percent of the time, and that's a conservative estimate.''

"That doesn't leave much time for anything else,'' Johanna protested.

Hunter silently applauded. "That's right. You figured it out. I'd guess ninety-eight percent of a man's brain is involved with thinking about—'' he gestured at his lap and leaned forward in an earnest fashion "—which leaves only two percent for everything else. This is why girls do better in school. They've got more of their brain available to devote to the task. The male animal, Johanna, especially the male adolescent animal, has one goal in life.''

"Oh, really?'' Johanna responded suspiciously. "I'm afraid to ask. What, pray tell, might that be?''

"To copulate with the world.'' He nodded at her. "It is the secret ambition of every boy over the age of about ten.''

"That's depraved.''

"That's real. Some of us are just a little better at hiding it than others so we don't scare you all off.''

"Even you?'' She knew there'd been something simmering below his surface. Hadn't she sensed it all along?

"Me?" Hunter pointed at his chest.

"Yeah."

"I'm almost thirty. Past my prime, you know? I figure I'm down to only ninety percent of my brain being preoccupied with sex, but it could be as low as eighty-eight, eighty-nine percent by now, I suppose."

Johanna simply stared. "This is simply amazing."

"Easy for you to say. You don't have to deal with it on a daily basis."

"Oh, yes I do. All right, it's a deal. Two Saturday afternoons of baby-sitting. But you have to talk to both Chris and Charlie and get them set straight."

"There may be some overtime involved," Hunter warned. "Depends on how deeply indoctrinated they are. Really strong testosterone barriers can be hard to break through, you know. I'll expect additional recompense if that turns out to be the case." He'd have Johanna wound around his unholy foursome's collective finger in no time at this rate because he hadn't made any of this up. Teenage boys were totally stuck on one subject—sex. Long before Charlie and Chris were under control he'd have to start working on Stephen and then Will. Yep, he had her, all right.

"Fine. Whatever it takes. Friday's my birthday. Bring the kids over after practice for cake and ice cream. You can talk to Charlie and Chris then."

It was mortifying to admit he had no plans for Friday night. There'd been a time in the not-so-distant past when he'd have had to whip out his electronic calendar and juggle things like crazy to try and fit something like this in—"three months from next Tuesday there was a possibility of maybe four to five minutes at two in the morning" kind of thing.

Not anymore.

He could talk about sex with her brothers from now until doomsday and not have it interfere with one darn thing on his social calendar. And the really sad part of it was talking about sex was a step above anything else he'd accomplished along those lines lately.

How the mighty were fallen.

Well, with any luck he'd be rectifying that soon.

"I think I can make that work," Hunter allowed. "And then I get all Saturday afternoon to myself." No harm in double-checking here. He sent up a little prayer that the kids would go with her, but Hunter was pretty sure they'd feel safe with Johanna.

"Right," Johanna agreed, and stood up. "What are you going to do with six whole hours unencumbered with children?"

"I've got technical reading I should be doing. I'd love to drive into Chicago and do even a couple of hours at a museum. It'd be great to go to a music store and pick out some hot CDs." A willing woman would also be good, but Hunter supposed now was not the time to mention that.

Johanna scooped up her books. She'd lived most of her life juggling seven schedules with her own. She recognized wishful thinking when she heard it. "So what'll you really do?"

Hunter sighed and prepared to leave himself. "Drop some suits at the dry cleaners, go to the hardware, the grocery and the pharmacy, then, time allowing, I'll reseat the toilet and pray that this time it won't leak, balance the checkbook and assemble the shelves I bought for Aaron and Mikie's room. Those two have the largest collection of mini cars and trucks I've ever seen, no lie."

"I can relate. I have this secret fantasy that someday I'm going to have time to soak myself until I'm pickled in a bubble bath," Johanna confessed. "Drink a piña colada while I do it. Read a book that has nothing to do with anything relevant in my life. But every time I get a little time to myself it seems there are a hundred and one things I need to do and it's all got to fit into a fifty-job time slot."

"I hear you," Hunter said with feeling. "The kids aren't

swimming tonight. Religious education classes,'' he explained. Oh, yes, Hunter had found religion, and if he had to find it, those little heathens were damn well going to find it, too. Fair was fair. "But I'll see you tomorrow."

"Right."

Johanna went to her last class of the day, then drove home. Once she got there, there were still forty-five minutes before the bus came and dumped off Stephen, Will and Aubrey. There was also four dozen cookies to make for Will's Cub Scout pack meeting tomorrow afternoon. Sighing, Johanna entered the kitchen. She removed two sticks of butter from the refrigerator, took off their wrappers and plopped them into a bowl to soften. Opening the cabinet under the sink, she went to deposit the wrappers into the trash receptacle hidden there.

"Darn it," she exploded. "Grace never emptied the trash." Leaning forward, Johanna craned her neck to look out the window over the sink. Head resting against the glass, she turned as far to the left as she could to catch the end of the driveway in her line of sight. "I don't think the trash men have come yet," she assured herself. "Maybe I can get it out in time." This was a major issue. There were eight people creating garbage in the house and the trash men came once a week. If the garbage didn't get put out, especially now with the warmer weather—yuck.

She raced out to the garage and pulled the cans down to the end of the drive so at least the majority of the trash would go, ran back into the house and started making the rounds to get the minor stuff that hadn't made it to the big curbside cans yet. The small baskets in all three bathrooms, the bag of lint from the laundry room and the almost-full bag from under the kitchen sink, all got dumped into one big bag. Once again she craned her neck at the window.

"Thank God they're running late today,'' she muttered, and raced back up the stairs. There was time for the bedrooms. The most important one was the wastebasket in the bedroom she shared with her mother. Quickly she upended it over the larger bag she'd been filling, but she was so hurried, she spilled it.

"Darn it, I don't have time for this," Johanna muttered as she scooped crumpled papers and broken pencils up and stuffed them into the bag she still needed to run out to the curb. She picked up a small crushed box and prepared to shove it after the rest when the writing on it caught her eye. "What's this?" Johanna asked herself as she read. "Early pregnancy test?"

Dumbfounded, Johanna stared at it. "Early pregnancy test?" she repeated. "Oh, my God."

Somebody in the house thought she might be pregnant.

Chapter Five

Johanna continued to stare in disbelief at the box. Seeing was believing, but this…this was, well, unbelievable.

But the evidence was right in front of her.

Somebody was pregnant. Or thought she was. In this house? Who?

Not her, that was for darn sure. Not unless you wanted to get into a second virgin birth kind of thing. No, it wasn't her. She wasn't holy enough. Not with the language she'd used last night.

The boys were out of the running for obvious reasons.

There was Grace and Aubrey. Ridiculous.

That left—her mother.

Off in the distance Johanna recognized the distinctive sounds of an approaching garbage truck. Instinctively she buried the box down inside the bag and raced through the house and out the garage entrance. There it was at the end of the block. Quickly she stuffed the bag into the curbside can, slapped the lid down over it as though to protect it from view, and ran back up to the house. Breathing hard she plunked herself down at the kitchen table.

Johanna put a hand to her forehead. What in the world was the matter with her? Like the trash man or the neighbors had X-ray vision or something and would know what she'd just deposited out there. "Good grief, get a grip, Jo." She needed to think. She needed food. Food helped you think. It was a known scientific fact. You had to feed your brain if you wanted it to work properly.

Feeling dazed, Johanna rose and went to the refrigerator. Digging way into the back of the freezer section, she pulled out several frozen snack-size Snickers from her hidden cache inside an old empty green bean bag. Ripping the wrapper off one, she bit into it. "Probably break a tooth," she mumbled around the candy as she poured herself a glass of milk.

Frozen Snickers and milk, the perfect comfort food, she thought as she sat heavily back down at the kitchen table.

Head supported by a hand on her forehead, Johanna chewed, swallowed and chased it down with a swallow of milk. "Think," she commanded herself. She reviewed the facts while she demolished the Snickers bars.

"All right now, the box was in the trash in the room I share with mother. I am not pregnant. That would be a medical miracle. No, it is not me."

The pile of candy wrappers grew rapidly. The cup of milk was half gone.

"Someone could have planted it there to avoid suspicion." She waved a candy bar in the air while she thought that one through. "So who? Aubrey thinks boys are a lower life-form, and not only has Ryan stopped speaking to Grace since she beat him at the last swim meet, she just got her first period a couple of weeks ago. I know. She was so sure she'd be the last one in the eighth grade to get it we had to celebrate with popcorn and root beer floats the fact that she'd beaten several of the other girls out.

"Stephen and Will not only can't get pregnant themselves but would rather die than talk to a girl.

"Chris and Charlie are pretty stupid but surely not so dumb as to hide a girlfriend's pregnancy test kit in their mother's wastebasket."

That left only one alternative.

"Mother? Pregnant?" But that would mean she'd been having sex. "Ridiculous. My mother would not have sex. Besides, who would she have it with?"

Her mother was forty-three years old, for God's sake. Unmarried forty-three-year-olds did not have sex, did they? "Of course not." At least not *her* mother. Presumably Maddie had put up with that kind of nonsense a few times when she was younger. "Much younger." After all, Johanna was one of seven and had seen her mother pregnant with her own two eyes. You couldn't argue with that kind of evidence even if it was hard to swallow.

But now the woman was forty-three and surely past all that stuff.

Besides, she was no longer married—not to anyone. Nobody at all.

Johanna felt like she'd taken a blow to the solar plexus. The world as she knew it had suddenly tipped on its axis. "What in the world is going on here?"

Johanna viewed her mother very differently when they sat down to eat dinner. Maddie was picking at her food. She reminded Johanna of a limp piece of lettuce. Her mother even had a lettucelike touch of green to her complexion. Johanna watched her mother close her eyes and swallow hard when William and Aubrey played *show* with a mouthful of meat loaf and mashed potatoes. Admittedly, it *was* fairly disgusting.

"Cut it out, you two. That's sick."

"It all gets mixed up in your stomach, anyway, Jo. That's what you always say when my gravy spreads out into the Jell-O or rolls."

"And it does. That doesn't mean anybody wants to see it."

Stephen stuck out a tongue full of chewed-up vegetables mixed with what—applesauce?—right at Johanna, and since she was seated next to her mother, Maddie got the full view. Her mother pushed back her chair and fled the table.

Johanna pointed a finger at her brother. "Okay, buster, that's ten minutes extra piano practice time for you."

"Making practice a punishment is hardly going to instill a love of music," Chris informed her.

"I have to listen to it, too, don't I?" Johanna shot back. "He's ruining *my* love of music, so why should he get off scot-free? And next time we go to the dentist, bring a book. All those parenting magazines you leafed through in the waiting room last time warped your mind."

With that parting shot Johanna pushed her own chair back and went after her mother. "And by the way, don't either you or Charlie make plans for tomorrow night. It's my birthday."

"What?"

"Hey, Jo, can't I like tell you happy birthday now? I made plans—"

"Unmake them. I've invited a guest lecturer. You'll love it."

"Oh, man, this is *so* not happening."

Johanna followed her mother up the stairs. "Mom? Mom?" The hall bathroom door was shut and a light shone underneath. She knocked on the door. "Mom? You okay in there?"

Maddie's voice drifted back through the wood panel. It sounded weak. "I'm fine, honey. Just a touch of flu, I think."

Yeah, the nine-month variety. Johanna listened as Maddie lost her dinner. "Mom?"

"Really," Maddie gasped. "Go on back down and finish eating."

Well golly gee whiz, what do you know? What with

everybody doing their best to gross one another out down there and listening to her mother throw up, Johanna had sort of lost her appetite. She leaned her head against the door panel and tried to think. She was twenty-four years old, twenty-five tomorrow, and her mother, her *unwed* mother was expecting.

Johanna shut her eyes. Then she opened them wide.

Good Lord in heaven. She was going to be on her own in just a few short weeks. She had job applications out. She'd been apartment hunting. Now her mother was having a baby. What would that do to her own plans? Oh, man. How could she possibly leave now?

Johanna went back downstairs in a daze. Maddie never showed back up. Johanna assumed she'd put herself to bed. At seven o'clock in the evening. Johanna oversaw the kitchen cleanup, practicing and homework, but her heart wasn't really in it. Naturally her siblings immediately sensed it and took advantage, doing a haphazard job of all three. Johanna looked at the floor she'd swear hadn't seen a broom, the countertop that had gotten maybe one swipe with a sponge and the homework paper with the handwriting that made hieroglyphics look good. She shook her head and went to bed herself.

She woke up on her twenty-fifth birthday seriously depressed.

"It would be cowardly to pull the sheet up over my head and never get up," she lectured herself sternly. But it was tempting. Oh, was it ever tempting.

"Get up," Johanna ordered. But she didn't. "Why should I listen to myself?" she asked. "God knows nobody else in this house does." Oh, good, now she was feeling sorry for herself. Johanna rolled her eyes in exasperation.

Fifteen minutes later she'd succeeded in rolling out of the bed, washing her face and pulling on jeans and a T-shirt. Pretty major accomplishments, all things considered.

Johanna made the rounds banging on doors. "Get up,

you guys. If I have to be up, so do you.'' There was a lot of mumbling and groaning, but the troops fell in line pretty quickly.

''Chris,'' she told her brother when he entered the kitchen, ''when you get home from school you need to bake a cake. Yellow. With penuche frosting. I do not want chocolate with Gummi Worms crawling out of it like last year, understand?''

''Jo, gifts should come from the heart,'' he informed her. ''If you tell me to bake you a birthday cake, it loses its meaning, and since you've already told me to do it, it's too late for me to offer, so I guess somebody else will have to do it.''

Johanna was going to personally order some teenage-type magazines for their dentist. Something dealing with hot cars rather than hot girls would be good. For sure she was going to vet the kid's reading material next time they were stuck in the waiting room for a teeth cleaning. ''Chris, I'll be eighty-five instead of twenty-five before any of you offers and you know it. I am not baking my own birthday cake.''

Now he stooped to whining. ''I always have to do everything. Why can't Charlie bake it?''

''Because we want to be able to eat it. Deal with it.''

''This is *so* not fair.''

Johanna thought about all the plans she'd made for her life and how they'd gone up in smoke the night before. And even that wasn't the first time she'd had to rearrange her life for her family. ''Tell me about it.''

Her mother came down, pale but dressed for work, in time to kiss the little ones goodbye. As the door slammed on the last one, Johanna said, ''Mom, we need to talk.''

''Can it wait? I'm running a bit late this morning. I fell back asleep after the alarm went off, I guess.''

Johanna's mouth tightened into a grim line. ''Mom, sit

down. This won't take long. You overslept. After going to
bed at seven o'clock last night?

"Now, Mom, you raised seven kids. You've lived
through food fights that left spinach hanging off the kitchen
light fixture.

"I watched while you fished the tip of Will's finger out
of his bicycle chain and took it to the hospital with him to
get it stitched back on.

"Then, last night, you suddenly get all squeamish over
a little bit of *show?*

"I don't think so, Mom."

"I told you, Jo, it's a touch of—"

"Mom, I found the box."

Johanna wouldn't have believed it possible, but her
mother paled even further. She was going to have to make
sure she had a blood test. She was probably anemic on top
of everything else. Terrific.

"Box?"

"I missed when I emptied the wastebasket in our bedroom. It fell out onto the floor. An early pregnancy home
test guaranteed to be ninety-eight percent accurate. You
may remember it. On the small side, blue with black writing?"

Maddie sat on the edge of a kitchen chair and studied
the tabletop. Avoiding Johanna's gaze she picked up toast
crumbs by pressing her fingertip to them.

"I know. The tabletop's dirty. I'm going to take care of
it as soon as we're done here. Mom, it's my birthday. I'm
a quarter of a century old today. Tell me you're not going
to announce you're having a baby."

Maddie spread her hands helplessly and her bottom lip
trembled slightly, which made Johanna's eyes begin to fill.
A child, no matter how old, was never more at a loss than
when they saw their parent cry.

"Johanna, for the first time in my life I don't know what

to do. The test was positive. I don't have the flu. I'm pregnant.''

Johanna had known it since she'd taken out the trash yesterday. Intellectually she'd had the information but emotionally she hadn't processed it until right now with her mother confirming it right to her face. What had she thought, a gremlin had come in and planted the evidence simply to stir up trouble? Johanna must have, because she felt as if she'd been dumped into Lake Michigan in the middle of a January ice storm. Icy fingers went down her back. Hell, icy arms were wrapped around her chest, squeezing. Johanna couldn't breathe, couldn't get any air at all.

Maddie rose, picked up her briefcase. "I can't think about this right now. When I think about it I—I have to go. I'm late." And she walked out the door leaving Johanna standing there.

Johanna could even understand her mother's reaction. She couldn't think about it, either. What did you do when you couldn't think? You went through the motions of normal life. You might feel like an automaton, but you kept going. Otherwise you'd curl up in a ball and scream your head off, which was pretty much what she felt like doing just then.

"Where's the sponge?" Johanna asked herself. "I need to wipe off the table. And the countertops. The sponge…" Helplessly she looked around the room before her eyes fastened on the sink. "The sponge is in the sink. Where else would it be? It's in the sink."

She'd crossed half the distance between the table and the sink when she came to a dead stop. You know what? Her mother wasn't all that holy, either. There was a man involved here somewhere. But who?

Johanna retrieved the sponge and wiped furiously while she thought. She worked one spot so long and so hard the countertop was in danger of wearing through.

To her knowledge, her mother did not date anyone. Certainly she'd never brought a man back to the house for Sunday dinner or to meet her children.

Fact two, Johanna knew Maddie had married young. Obviously. She'd had seven children by age thirty-six and there was only one set of Irish twins in the bunch. Also of interest, Chuck Durbin had been the third guy Maddie had even dated. Maddie had told her so. Given that, what would her mother know about men and their sly, underhanded ways?

Johanna finally realized she'd washed the same section of countertop about one hundred and ten times. She moved back to the sink, rinsed out the sponge and chose a different stretch of counter to torture.

"Maybe it was someone from the office. Didn't I read somewhere about male bosses holding a woman's job over her head if she didn't sleep with them?" Sexual harassment in the workplace. Now, that was a likely possibility here, because Johanna knew that her mother would never knowingly, willingly—oh, God, it didn't bear thinking about. First her brother and now her mother. Was the whole world obsessed with sex?

Using one arm to support herself, Johanna leaned over the sink. She dropped the sponge back in, then covered her eyes with her hands. She needed to talk to someone. Life was getting to be a bit heavy-duty and she needed a sounding board. Basically Johanna wanted somebody to dump on, someone to hold her and hug her and tell her everything was going to be all right. She didn't even have to mentally go through her list of friends.

She wanted Hunter.

And that little bit of self-realization shook her every bit as badly as the news of her mother's pregnancy.

Naturally she'd been aware of him as a man since the moment she'd first slapped eyes on him. Hunter Pace would make a good addition to any hospital. Think your patient's slipped over the edge but want to make sure? Put Hunter in the room with her. If his mere presence didn't bring a blood pressure spike, then if she wasn't already dead she was the next closest thing to it and not worth worrying over.

So yes, he made her heart race, her breasts tingle and her feminine sheath pulse. Good news. She wasn't dead. She also wasn't shallow like her brother Charlie. There was more to Hunter than a great body that could make the dead sit up and take note.

Not that Johanna didn't want the body because she did. *She* wasn't in her forties and somebody's, actually several somebodies' mother, for God's sake. It was okay for her to want.

But the wanting wasn't all there was to it. No, there was a depth to Hunter that made the wanting all the more dangerous. Johanna couldn't ignore the pull she felt, couldn't just write it off as a meaningless hormone thing and wait for it to pass like an attack of hay fever after the first frost. Who did she most want to talk this through with? Hunter. Not her best friend Lisa or her psychology professor at IUSB. Hunter. And that was scary. In her heart of hearts Johanna just knew something strong could develop here. A long, lasting relationship kind of thing.

That she didn't like, not even the idea. Here she'd been just about to spread her wings and fly. She didn't *want* to meet the man of her dreams. Not yet.

And then there were his niece and nephews. Cute, sure, but wouldn't it be just her luck if Hunter had them permanently? What if the parents weren't stationed in the Mideast or wherever? What if—God forbid—they weren't coming back at all? Her heart contracted for a moment at the thought of those four children being orphaned. Then she realized they would never really be alone as long as good old Uncle Hunter was around.

Good grief.

Hunter could be *raising* those children. All *four* of those children.

"Wouldn't that just be the corker?" Johanna asked herself.

She spent the day worrying herself half to death. Johanna knew it was only halfway because when she got to swim practice and Hunter winked at her from the stands her blood pressure spiked. Heck, she'd have to not only be dead but buried for a month or two before any physiological response to the man's mere presence stopped. Damn but he was gorgeous. And he truly seemed interested in her. Go figure.

Johanna smiled back and then determinedly gave her attention to the little ones in her care.

"Okay, everybody, we're going to practice starts. Everybody line up."

"Can I be first, Coach Jo?"

"He got to be first last time. I wanna be first."

Hunter watched while Johanna ruthlessly organized her team. Before he could blink the squabbling had stopped and little bodies hurtled themselves off the starting block at Johanna's signal.

"Take your mark, *hup!*

"Take your mark, *hup!*"

What a woman.

"Uncle Hunter?"

"What, Aaron?" Hunter never took his eyes off Johanna as he absently answered the four-year-old.

"Mikie's gotta go potty."

"Hmm?" Just look at the arch of Johanna's throat when she threw her head back and laughed at something one of the kids said. She was so *alive* it made a man's mouth go dry just watching her.

"Mikie's gotta go potty *bad,* Uncle Hunter."

That got his attention. Mikie's success at making the

toilet was hit or miss. "What? How can you tell?" His alarmed gaze swung from Johanna's lithe form to his nephew. "Mikie, do you have to go to the bathroom?" The answer was obvious. Mikie was holding himself and dancing a little jig for all he was worth. Hunter picked him up, holding him out at arm's length just in case, and ran for it. "Come on, Aaron, you, too. I'm not leaving either one of you alone for even a moment here. Next thing I know you'll be going for another swim. Move! Mikie, you're supposed to tell me when you need the bathroom, remember?"

It was nip and tuck but twenty minutes later Hunter settled back onto the hard metal bench with a sigh of relief. Crisis averted. He'd left the house in a rush without a spare pair of training pants and shorts for Mikie, but they'd just made it. He ought to start keeping an extra set in his car. What a great idea! He'd get the hang of this parenting stuff, just see if he didn't. Hunter grimaced as Mikie and Aaron each picked up a Matchbox car and raced them up and down his leg. Predictably there was a major pileup on his shin.

"Ouch. Take it easy, guys. Uncle Hunter's got to walk when this is all over."

"Uncle Hunter?"

"Yeah?"

"I gotta go potty."

"Aaron, we just came back from the bathroom. Why didn't you go when Mikie went?" What a stupid question. Why didn't the sun and moon synchronize their orbits? Because. Just because. And, in fact, Aaron simply shrugged. It was evidently one of those inexplicable laws of nature. No two little boys will ever go to the bathroom at the same time and place. Unless it was someplace inconvenient or totally inappropriate. Then they'd all happily pee their little hearts out.

Hunter sighed and rose. "Come on. Let's go."

Practice finally ended. Johanna had been very cognizant of Hunter watching from the stand. It had made her self-conscious and time had dragged. With a sigh of relief she passed out her birthday cupcakes and sent all her little ones off to the locker room. They left a trail of chocolate cake crumbs behind them. She shook her head as she noticed it. You know, she'd actually miss the little stinkers when she quit this job. Why, Johanna couldn't begin to imagine. God knew she'd overdosed on young children years ago. Nevertheless it was the truth. She'd miss them. Each and every rotten one of them.

Hunter came down from the bleachers to meet her, Aaron and Mikie attached like little limpets. "Hi," he said, and raked a hand through his hair. There'd been another pileup on top of his head. His hair was probably sticking straight up. He'd always had this one cowlick that specialized in giving him grief. He could just imagine what a car crash in the near vicinity had done to it.

"Hi, yourself," Johanna responded, grinning stupidly. "You've almost got it." She reached up and patted a spike of hair back into place.

"Thanks."

"You're welcome."

They stood staring at each other.

Hunter hunched his shoulders, feeling slightly foolish. "So, how's it going?"

Eagerly Johanna jumped on the conversation gambit. "Good. It's going good. You?"

Hunter nodded equably. "Oh, good. You, uh, going to swim tonight?" Please? He could use another dose of seeing Johanna in a swimsuit. In fact, he'd been looking forward to it all day. That mental image had been his one saving grace several times during an interminably long day.

"No. Not tonight. I put Charlie and Chris in charge of cleaning up the kitchen and getting everything ready for the cake and ice cream. I need to take the younger four home since Charlie and Chris are busy preparing for my party, ha ha.''

"Ah." Well, damn. You're out of luck, Pace.

"As soon as they're dressed, you can follow me."

Hunter pushed his hands into his pockets and rocked on his heels. "Sounds like a plan." He gestured to the empty pool with a nod of his head. "You're good with them."

Johanna's gaze turned to the clear water. "Thanks. They're good kids. Make you crazy at times, but they're all good kids."

He understood perfectly. His four were good as gold— for kids—and they had him half insane.

They chatted briefly about Karen and Robby's swim progress, how they were fitting into their new school. They discussed the difficulty Hunter had avoiding making comparisons when the children were so close, age-wise. Robby's indifference to reading was going to have to be overcome, while Karen was passing Robby in reading skills. They covered Aaron's odd attachment for a certain cup at mealtime and Mikie's staying dry all day.

Hunter was startled when Karen, Robby and Johanna's four younger siblings converged on the pool area. He was also mortified. Good grief, he'd just spent a good twenty minutes one-on-one with a beautiful woman discussing *children*. Hunter barely refrained from smacking his own forehead. It had only been a couple of months. Was he becoming a parent or what?

"Everybody got everything?" Johanna asked. They all nodded. She wasn't budging without going through the checklist. She'd made too many return runs to trust them.

"Suit? Towel? Soap, shampoo back in a sealed bag so they can't leak on anything?"

"Yeah, yeah, yeah. We got it all, Jo. Let's go. We want cake.''

"Don't yeah, yeah me, Grace," Johanna warned. "Who was it left her music at her piano lesson and didn't even notice for three days? Says a lot about the quality of your practicing, doesn't it? Open your bags and double-check." She looked at their feet. They still wore their poolside flip-flops. "Make sure your shoes are in there, too. And not one but two socks."

They groaned but knew their sister wouldn't budge until they'd cooperated. Dutifully they knelt on the concrete, opened their bags and cursorily rooted through them. "Yep, all here. Just like we said."

What a great idea, Hunter thought, and opened Karen and Robby's bag and pulled a few things out. "Where are your goggles?"

"Oops."

"Run get them." Robby took off for the locker room. Several minutes later he was back.

"I guess that about does it," Hunter said. He turned to Johanna. "Lead the way." Then he took her arm to guide her to the parking lot.

Johanna immediately turned red at the gentlemanly gesture. Grace giggling and elbowing Stephen didn't help matters. Through the embarrassment still came a deep-seated awareness of the man walking beside her. No other man of her acquaintance could make her arm tingle simply by touching it.

Johanna drove the minivan home. She was twenty-five and single. What was she doing driving a minivan? Transporting four children, that's what. She sighed and pulled into the garage.

Hunter pulled up the drive behind her and parked his flashier two-door in the turnaround behind her. He supposed he ought to get one of those minivans like Johanna drove. Be roomier for the kids, he thought glumly, more safety belts. Just last night some lady, Billy somebody's mother, had approached him wanting to know where he lived and whether he'd be interested in carpooling. Carpooling! Him! Life had reached a new all-time low. Damn, he was going to hate giving up this little gem. Lovingly he patted the hood as he circled around it.

Johanna ushered them all into the house. Her whole family awaited. They'd hung torn strips of varying lengths of crepe paper streamer fashion in the doorway and inflated balloons were stuck everywhere.

"You guys didn't use tape on the walls, did you?" she asked Charlie.

"Nah, we rubbed 'em on our shirts till they got good and electric and stuck them on the wall with static electricity."

She nodded her approval. "Great. Thanks. Everything looks great. It's the best birthday present you could have given me."

"Good, 'cuz I didn't have money to get you a real one."

"That's okay. To have everything ready like this is better."

Charlie nodded acceptance of her praise as his due.

"I got you a real present, Jo," Grace assured her.

"Did you, honey? If you picked it out I know I'm going to love it."

"I didn't have any money but I made you a card all by myself."

Johanna pulled Aubrey in for a one-armed body hug. "Thank you, sweetie. I'm going to put it in my memory box and save it."

"Yeah, well I made my card on the computer so it's really cool," Will said, not wanting to be outdone by his younger sister.

Johanna leaned over and kissed his forehead. "I'm saving yours, too, Will, not to worry."

Will scrubbed at his forehead. "Okay."

Hunter and his troops were quickly assimilated into the chaotic scene. They all sang happy birthday, and the kids added an embarrassing second verse that demanded to know her boyfriend's first name. Then they insisted she actually answer.

"You guys know I don't have a boyfriend."

"Oh, yeah?" They all hooted and hollered. "Then who's that?" and they pointed right at Hunter.

Hunter, not about to let a good opportunity go to waste, stepped forward. "Yeah, who am I?" He leaned her back over his arm and kissed her Rudolph Valentino style, which sent the crowd into an additional frenzy. To the single-digit age group, nothing was quite so pleasingly disgusting as two people kissing.

"Happy birthday," he said.

"Do it again, Uncle Hunter, kiss her again."

"Did you see that?" Will demanded of nobody in particular. "Oh, man, that is so *gross.*"

Her mother watched with a small smile on her face while Chris and Charlie looked anywhere but at Johanna and Hunter. Now, *that* was funny. The sexual liberators of the teenage crowd were embarrassed seeing their sister get a birthday kiss.

Johanna caught Hunter's gaze and tipped her head in Chris and Charlie's direction.

He nodded and sighed. Here went nothing. Man, he had truly crossed the great divide. He, Hunter Pace, was about to give a talk on responsible sex, instead of being on the receiving end. He was officially old.

Chapter Six

Johanna read her cards and opened her presents while Hunter plotted his next move.

"Ooh, Aubrey, great card. I'm going to put it up on the mantel so everyone can admire it. Yours, too, Will."

He didn't know how to talk about responsible sex with a couple of adolescent boys he'd just met. Was he crazy? No, desperate. Hunter shrugged. Same thing.

"Thanks, Mom. It'll be great having brand-new towels when I set up housekeeping. And blue is my favorite color."

"We know," all her siblings chorused together.

"Everything you own is blue," Chris snickered.

"Not everything."

"Almost."

See? Some good could come of this. Now he knew her favorite color, a fact that didn't get his job done. Okay, so how to play this? Buddy-buddy?

Dubiously he eyed the duo he was to deal with and discarded that option. He'd come too far from those days and had no intention of even pretending to go back.

Intimidation was always good. Do it my way or I'll re-arrange your face kind of thing. He was big enough, but he suspected that type of approach would simply garner resentment rather than compliance. Hunter massaged his temples with his fingers and worried whether he was becoming prone to migraines.

He avoided eye contact with Johanna while he tossed paper plates into the trash and helped clean up. Then he shepherded the youngest ones out the back door to play on the swing set and sandbox he'd noticed from the kitchen window. Initially Hunter sat on the back steps to watch them, then noticed the basketball hoop. Fishing his keys out of his pocket he counted the children, then carefully backed his car down the driveway, making sure the kids all stayed in front of him. He grabbed a basketball from the grassy area behind the standard and started doing layups while he brooded.

Johanna watched from the window over the kitchen sink. She took a final swipe to clean the faucet itself, dropped the sponge and went out to join him. She'd played some intramural in high school—never made the actual school team, but she was good enough to harass him a bit, make him work for his shots. It didn't take long for the taunts to start.

"Come on, Jo, go around him. You can do better than that. He's too large to be fast."

"Hey, big guy, you gonna let a *girl* score on you like that?"

Hunter, who'd been holding back to make more of a game of it, merely smiled. "What can I say? She's tough."

"How about if Chris and I take you two on?" Charlie called.

Hunter dribbled thoughtfully. "A little two-on-two?"

Charlie shrugged innocently. "Why not?"

Jumping lightly, Hunter casually tossed the ball in the general direction of the basket from twenty feet out. The ball swished through, catching nothing but net. "I guess that'd be okay."

Johanna's eyes widened, then she grinned. "We're gonna kick your butts," she crowed.

Only just then a plaintive cry came from the sandbox. "Jo, I've got sand in my eye. Come quick," Aubrey called. "It hurts really, really bad." Johanna had to leave the makeshift court to help Aubrey flush her eye out.

"Well, that takes care of that," Charlie said, his voice disgusted.

"Why do you say that?" Hunter asked. "I'll take you both on," he offered. "You guys being such jocks and all, you'll probably clobber me, me being so old and everything." Hunter bounced the ball temptingly, then spun it on the tip of his index finger.

Charlie eyed the spinning ball narrowly. "It wouldn't be fair. Two on one like that, I mean."

Hunter let the ball run down his arm, across the top of his shoulders, then along his other arm. He flipped it into his left hand. "Why don't we just see?"

"Look at him," Chris said with a poke of his elbow into Charlie's gut. "He's settin' us up, man. Look at the way he's handling the ball." Just then Hunter spun around, arched one arm up high and let the ball fly. Again he caught nothing but net.

"I know," Charlie whispered back. "I've got eyes. You gonna be the one to tell him that the two of us don't want to play because we're afraid one old guy is gonna beat us? He's good, but there are two of us. We can take him."

"Oh, man."

Now Charlie jabbed Chris back with an elbow. "Quit whining and let's do it. You guard him. Stay right in his face. I'll handle the shooting. All right," Charlie said louder. "We'll take you on." He immediately began trash-talking. "And don't worry. Chris and I both know CPR. We'll know what to do when you have your heart attack."

"There's a relief," Hunter grunted, and took the ball to the end of the turnaround to bring it in from out of bounds and begin play.

"Concentrate," Charlie yelled at Chris as Hunter came right at the younger brother, pivoted around him and sank in a three-pointer.

Now Charlie took the ball back to the end of the turnaround and passed it in bounds to Chris, only Chris never got his hands on it. Hunter intercepted the pass and went in for another two points. Thirty hot, sweaty minutes later, a half an hour broken only by the sharp slap of bouncing ball against concrete along with some grunting, groaning and mild cussing, Charlie and Chris admitted defeat. They collapsed, moaning on the cool green grass bordering the driveway and turnaround.

"Man, I'm dead," Chris groaned.

"Me, too," Charlie admitted. A shadow passed over him and he glared up. "You cheated."

Hunter dribbled the ball, alternating hands while he wished like crazy he wouldn't lose face if he, too, collapsed on the grass. "How so?"

"You let us think you weren't that good. Man, you could have played pro."

Hunter laughed at that. "Nah, but I was second string at the University of Michigan. We made final four my senior year. We had the lead by enough that the coach let me in for five minutes in the last quarter."

"Awesome."

"Yeah, awesome, dude."

Hunter wiped the sweat off his forehead with his shirtsleeve. "I need a drink of water," he muttered. "Then maybe Grace could watch the kids until Johanna gets back out here. I promised her I'd talk to you guys."

"Oh, man."

"I promised," he repeated grimly, and wished he could moan himself.

"Couldn't you, like, pretend? Say you talked to us? It's not like we haven't heard it all a million times from Jo and my mom."

"Evidently it hasn't sunk in." Hunter extended a hand to each boy and hauled them to their feet. "Come on, we're all men here. We can deal with this. Let's get it over with so I can report in and take my crew home."

"This is *so* something I don't want to hear," Chris complained. "Look at this, Charlie, she's even got *him* cowed."

"Needling isn't going to work," Hunter informed him as he turned the spigot controlling the hose on and drank thirstily. "A promise is a promise."

Charlie rolled his eyes and took the hose from Hunter, splashing his overheated red face first, then drinking from it in long, noisy gulps. "Make it quick, then. I already know all about sex. What I don't know is why everybody acts like it's so evil. I think they're just jealous 'cuz I've got somebody and they don't. Or maybe it's selfish. They want to keep the fun all to themselves. I mean, where's the harm? It feels great, and so long as you use something—"

"Maybe you know about sex," Hunter countered, "the mechanics of it, but you don't know squat about making love."

"Same thing," Charlie said, and passed the hose on to Chris.

"No," Hunter said, begging to differ, "it's not." He gestured toward the street. "Let's walk." After arranging for Grace to keep an eye on the sandbox crew, Hunter ushered the two boys out onto the pavement. Shoving his hands deep into his pockets, he brooded, searching in his mind for just the right opening.

"Hey, like we already surrendered," Chris said after a couple of blocks. "Slow down, man. What, are we doing a marathon now?"

"Hmm? Oh, sorry."

"Yeah, dude, just say it, will you? Geez, I thought *I* was a jock."

Hunter slowed his pace and took a deep breath. "Your sister asked me to talk to you two about sex and making love," he began slowly.

Charlie rolled his eyes. "This is all Aub's fault. If she hadn't blabbed—"

"The blabbing is not the problem," Hunter countered.

"Neither is the other. Everybody I know—"

"Everybody?"

"Almost everybody, okay? They're all active, I know it. It's not like a big secret or anything. They talk about it. How much fun it is and everything."

"You believe everything you hear in the locker room?"

"Why shouldn't I?" Charlie said defensively. "The guys wouldn't lie."

"Uh-huh. Any of the girls in that high school of yours pregnant?"

"Well, yeah, but they're the stupid ones."

"In other words, their boyfriends had nothing to do with their condition?"

Charlie scratched his forehead. Nothing like logic to give a teenage boy a headache. "I suppose so, but—"

"No buts about it. Let's put it another way. What do you think would happen if, for example, Johanna got pregnant right now?"

Chris hooted, "No way, man. She'd have to, like, let a guy near her first and that would never happen."

"Don't count on it," Hunter said under his breath. There was nothing he wanted more than to get close to Johanna Durbin, and he was damn well going to make sure it happened. "What would happen?" he repeated.

"The world would end," Charlie said facetiously.

"This'll go a whole heck of a lot faster if you guys cooperate here."

"Okay, fine. The world would not end. She'd have a

baby.'' Charlie shrugged. "Big deal. She'd have to get a job, find some day care, stuff like that. If she twisted his arm hard enough the guy might even marry her. Maybe. So what's your point?''

"What kind of job would she get, do you suppose?''

"Hell, I don't know. She wants to be some kind of social worker or something. Work with juvenile delinquents or underprivileged kids. Something like that.''

That surprised Hunter. He'd have thought she got enough of that at home, but he nodded agreeably, anyway. "So it'd be a decent job. She'd be able to support herself and the baby.''

"Like I said, it'd be no big deal other than the event of the miracle itself.''

Chris snorted his appreciation of that.

"Of course,'' Charlie continued, "social workers don't make all that much even with their college degrees. I don't know why she picked something like that in the first place. I'm going to start off at the Purdue branch here, but then I'm going down to West Lafayette and finish up at the main campus. Engineering. There are some bucks there. I don't want to struggle like Jo's going to have to.''

Now they were getting someplace. "Uh-huh. So, what are Molly's plans after high school?''

Charlie gave him an odd look, evidently puzzled by the non sequitur. "What? Molly? I don't know.''

"She going to college?''

Charlie shrugged. "I don't know. We never talked about it. I kind of doubt it. I don't think her grades are all that high. What difference does it make?''

"Just that not everybody in this area goes on. For some, high school is the extent of their formal education. It wouldn't overly upset them if they found themselves or their girlfriends pregnant and had to get married at seventeen or eighteen. It was the logical next step for them, anyway.''

"If *that's* what Jo's worried about, you can tell her, no problem. In fact, I'll tell her myself." Charlie halted in his tracks and pointed at his chest. "'Cuz *I'd* be upset. *I* have plans. I use a rubber. I take responsibility."

Hunter lifted a shoulder negligently. "All I'm saying is that mistakes happen. All it takes is one little runaway soldier and poof, there go all your plans, buddy. Unlike Johanna, you've got a ways to go before you could get a job that paid decently. Anything happened right now between you and Molly and guess who'll be flipping burgers in a fast-food joint or bagging in a grocery store for the rest of his life? Maybe both at the same time. Lots of people with low-paying jobs have to work more than one to support their families." Hunter eyed the boys, trying to decide if he was getting through at all.

"You know, my brother was supposed to be an only child because my mom was so sick with him," Hunter continued, "I faked them out, however, but it was no big deal. Timing, my friend, is everything in life. They were already married, already working, already stable." He paused, studied their expressions and then continued, "Sex is fun, you're right. It feels darn good, but it is not without its possible consequences. You ready to pay the bill for your pleasure?"

Charlie scowled, not liking the way the conversation was going. "So I'll double up. Wear two."

That ought to be interesting, thought Hunter. "You could give it a try, I suppose," he allowed. "Chris, you're being awfully quiet. You with us on any of this?"

"Yeah, I've been listening."

Charlie was getting impatient. He wasn't winning the argument so he saw no purpose in prolonging it. "So, like, are we done now? Can we go back? I've got a date with Molly. I'm already late and—"

"No, we're not done yet."

Charlie and Chris both sighed gustily. Hunter smiled

grimly. He wasn't exactly having a good time, either. He was damned uncomfortable in more ways than one. It had been a mistake conjuring up a picture of Johanna pregnant. He had already embellished it in his mind's eye. She was not only pregnant, but it was *his* child she carried. The mere mental image had the fit of his jeans tightening up considerably, which was ludicrous considering the way he was overrun with children as it was.

"Now we're going to talk about the difference between having sex and making love."

"Oh, man, do we have to?"

"Yes." Hunter could use a review himself. He'd definitely been having a lot of prurient thoughts himself lately.

"Women," Hunter began cautiously, "don't think the same as men."

Genuinely bewildered, Charlie asked, "Who cares what they think? The issue is whether they look hot or not."

Chris snickered. "Yeah, besides, they don't think. Just look at Johanna and Grace. And I don't think Aubrey's got a brain at all. Man, I killed her at Scrabble the other night."

"On the one hand," Hunter continued, doggedly refusing to be drawn into a comment on the fairness of a vocabulary contest between a sixteen-year-old and a seven-year-old, "men tend to think very linearly. We're fairly straightforward in our mental processes and, as a matter of fact, in our bodies. We see, we want, our body automatically and rather blatantly readies itself to take. Women, on the other hand, well, they're a little more convoluted in their approach to life. Uh, they tend to get all tangled up in a bunch of emotional stuff." He stopped to rub his nose. "Where as we can rise above all that junk, they can't, okay? They trip on it, scrape their mental knee and bang their psychological elbow. Or worse." Hunter struggled a bit before continuing. "I guess it boils down to this. A guy your age thinks he's having sex while the girl is positive she's making love. In other words, her emotions are all

tangled up in what you see as a fairly straightforward physical operation. Meanwhile she thinks she's in love. They
think they're the superior ones because they have this in-
bred ability to *look below the surface*. Let me think, what
else do they call it? Oh, yeah, they also *read between the
lines*. *You* haven't said anything at all but *they* know better.
Then everybody's surprised when the female ends up all
hurt with these bruised emotions and weeping all over the
guy.''

''Molly doesn't—''

''Molly may not even realize it herself, but Molly does.''

''Oh, man. That is like *so* not true.''

Hunter knew that was what Charlie desperately wanted
to believe, at any rate. He continued. ''Which means if you
take advantage of her feelings just so you can scratch an
itch you've got, so to speak, well then, that makes you a
user.''

''That is like *so* not what is happening between us. I
have never told Molly I loved her.''

''You don't have to open your mouth. Every time you
touch her intimately she's hearing you say it, clear as day.''

''What?''

''I'm serious, kid. Women are weird. Molly is making
assumptions based on your actions. You wouldn't be wanting to do those things with her if you didn't love her. That's
what she's thinking, Charlie. I guarantee it. And the more
intimate you get with her, the more assumptions she's going to make.''

Chris looked thoughtful.

Charlie complained loudly, ''I don't believe this.''

Hunter pressed his point. ''It's the truth. You care for
this girl enough to marry her, have children with her, spend
the rest of your life with her?''

''Hell, no. I mean, she's hot and everything, but I don't
even know who all she's slept with. I mean, I'm pretty sure

Jason Hartney was one, at least he *says* he's one, and anybody'd who'd sleep with him—''

"In other words, you're using her.''

Charlie stumbled all over himself. "Well, I mean...that is...she's *hot*."

"A man who *is* a man doesn't use, Charlie," Hunter replied quietly. "That's all I have to say. Let's go back. I need to get my own crew dunked in a tub and then dumped in bed. I've still got a lot of work to do tonight. And there's another thing you need to remember. A lifetime of baths, bedtime stories and carpooling is the logical conclusion of this kind of activity. Enough said." He slapped them both on the back. "Good game, guys. I enjoyed it. We'll have to do it again sometime soon."

"Yeah, right," Charlie groused, thoroughly disgruntled again. "I can hardly wait for you to come back and beat us, then rain all over my social life again. Thanks a bunch."

"Hey, no prob. That's what friends are for, right?" Hunter, trailed by two silent but hopefully thoughtful adolescents, retraced his steps back to Johanna's house.

They went in through the kitchen door.

"Hey," said Hunter, spying Johanna at the kitchen table.

"Hey yourself," she responded, looking up from her book.

"Thanks for ruining everything," Charlie snarled as he stomped by the table. "You are such a loser, Jo."

"Yeah, thanks a lot, Jo," Chris said with far less heat but evidently feeling obliged to close ranks with his brother against the reigning female.

Johanna's eyes widened and she turned to stare at her brothers' receding backs. "What was that all about?" she asked, turning back to Hunter.

"I think I got your point across successfully," he informed her. "You can't expect them to be grateful."

"No, I suppose not."

"What'd you do with the kids? It's so quiet. Did you gag them all and stick them in a closet somewhere?"

Johanna grinned at that. There'd been times over the past few years when the idea of a gag had held definite appeal. "They're in the family room playing Candy Land. I can't quite tell, but I think Mikie may be color-blind."

"Nah," Hunter scoffed, "he mixes up all his colors, not just red and green." But he'd look into it. "What're you doing?" He indicated the open book on the tabletop with a nod of his head.

"Getting an early start studying for finals." Johanna gestured at the book. "Abnormal psych."

"Ah," Hunter nodded wisely. "Useful stuff around that group you lead at the pool."

She grinned again. "Yeah."

Hunter turned one of the kitchen chairs around, straddled it and sat next to her. It would be harder to jump on her with the chair back between them. Suddenly it was important that he not be labeled a user himself. Important to him. For while it would have been much cleaner to simply have sex with Johanna, it was not what he wanted, not what he needed. Suddenly Hunter knew with blinding clarity that when he and Johanna came together it wouldn't be sex. It would be the much more complex and demanding process of making love. She deserved it, and come to think of it, so did he. He, thank God, was no longer seventeen.

Hunter rubbed his nose. Introspection irritated him. "So, you're going to be a social worker?"

"That was the plan," she muttered.

"You have the most beautiful eyes."

That brought her up short. "What?"

Good grief, how had he gotten sidetracked like that? "Nothing. Uh, let me think, oh, yeah, social work, that was it." He couldn't help himself. "But you do, you know. Have beautiful eyes."

Johanna blinked. Her eyes were brown. Plain, ordinary brown. "Thank you. I always wished they'd been blue."

"No," he said seriously. "Blue would be all wrong for you. Too cold. Your eyes are a wonderful warm golden brown. They suit you perfectly."

Johanna was ill at ease with compliments. Always had been. "Sort of like a well-done cookie?"

"One still hot from the oven," Hunter stipulated with a smile. She probably thought he was an idiot. He couldn't believe he'd blurted it out in the first place. "All I need is a glass of milk and I could eat you right up."

There was no light comeback to that. At least none Johanna could think of. It wasn't the most poetic of compliments she'd ever had. Actually, yes it was because she suspected it came from the heart. Hunter Pace wanted to eat her right up. She didn't think they'd gone through all the milk at suppertime. There ought to be at least another gallon in the backup refrigerator in the basement. Um, wait a just a minute here. "Uh—"

"Yeah, I know. Wrong time, wrong place. My timing used to be better." In a different lifetime. He sighed, glanced around. "You say the kids are in the family room? Maybe I could just take a few nibbles? You know, a little something to hold me over."

Johanna realized she'd been holding her breath, and exhaled. Mesmerized, she stared up into his own brilliant blue eyes. According to Hunter, blue eyes were cold. He'd obviously never looked closely into a mirror. His eyes weren't cold. No, they burned clear through right to her soul. Laser eyes. Blue flame burned the hottest, so they said. Johanna made a conscious effort to remember to breathe. If she kept stopping like this, she'd be passed out cold before much longer.

Hunter watched the play of emotions cross her face and knew Johanna was, in all likelihood, *reading between the lines*. Know what? He wanted her to. His kids could use a

mother, but not just any women would do any longer, for
Hunter had begun to suspect that what he himself needed—
and he was well aware of the verb change—was Johanna.
He leaned forward. Darned if he wasn't going to add to the
text of unspoken lines Johanna could read between.

"This probably isn't a good idea," Johanna murmured
before their lips could meet.

"It's not only a good idea, it's a great idea," Hunter
contradicted with great feeling.

And he set about to prove it.

He scootched his chair forward, leaning over the chair
back. She swayed forward, her hungry eyes on his mouth.
Oh, yeah, Johanna wanted this, too. Hunter didn't want
anything here to be one-sided. Pleased, he brushed her
mouth gently with his. Her lips were soft beneath his and
Hunter felt a sudden rush of protectiveness. He needed to
be careful. Things this soft could be easily crushed if
treated carelessly. Hunter vowed then and there to never
treat Johanna carelessly.

Again he brushed her lips carefully with his own, this
time slanting his head slightly. She'd been eating something
sweet. Hunter couldn't quite identify the flavor, but he
wanted more of it, yes, he most certainly did. So far he'd
managed to keep his hands locked on the chair back and
off of Johanna, but when she murmured a small inarticulate
protest as the kiss ended, the low sound threatened to break
his self-control into little pieces.

He scootched the chair forward another couple of inches
and brought his hands to rest on her shoulders. He used
them to gently guide Johanna forward once more. "You
are so beautiful," he murmured as he carefully tugged.

"Yeah," Johanna responded in a desperate bid to lighten
the suddenly heavy mood. "But am I hot?"

"Oh, yeah," Hunter vowed fervently. "Charlie doesn't
see it because he's your brother, but trust me on this. You
are definitely hot and I want you badly."

Her answering smile was fleeting. She closed her eyes and turned up her face. It was like turning it up to the sun as Hunter began to kiss her forehead, her cheeks, the tip of her nose. She went warm all over.

"Nobody else has ever thought so," she whispered, shivering when he dipped his tongue into her ear.

"They're blind," he assured her. "Every one of them is blind. And I'm glad of it. I'd get tired of having to beat them all off with a stick."

Johanna looked at him seriously. "Is that what you'd do?"

"Yes," he declared firmly, letting his hands skim lightly down her arms. "Johanna, you've been so busy and your brothers are, well, they're brothers. They're not about to build up your ego. I suspect plenty of guys noticed but you just never realized it. Guys are insecure, too, you know. They're not going to pursue without a little reciprocation from you. You're not the type to smile and flirt." Hunter took her hands and placed them on his shoulders so she'd have something to cling to. He intended to rattle her senses until she needed the support.

"I've got to tell you, Hunter, I don't feel much like smiling right now, either."

"I sincerely hope not," Hunter responded. With one hand he tipped her head back, then set about gently ravaging the slender throat he'd exposed.

"Oh, my," Johanna said on a quiet sigh.

"Yeah," Hunter agreed, only he would have shouted it with a whole lot more adverbs and adjectives.

"You're pretty good at this," she said, tipping her head back farther.

"Some things come better with age," Hunter said. "For kids like Charlie, it's a race to the finish. Can't do that with you."

"No?"

"No. Couldn't even if I wanted to. You're like a fine

wine, Johanna. Gulping it's a waste. You need to be savored, and that's just what I intend to do.''

"Yes," she agreed on a murmur, her eyes sliding shut. "And I want to savor you, too."

"Let's lose the chair," Hunter growled, and he stood to push the chair he'd been straddling out of his way.

Johanna, her hands still clasping his shoulders, rose with him. It was that or tumble face-first out of her own seat.

Hunter supported her while he wrestled with the furniture, then tugged her into his arms once the impediments had been removed. His hands slipped up under her shirt back, his fingers playing with the back of her bra while his mouth slanted down over hers. The temperature in the room seemed to rise several degrees. Hunter was sure the rise came from the heat of their embrace. There was a serious danger of spontaneous combustion in his estimation, and Hunter wondered if there was an automatic sprinkler system in the house, then shrugged the concern off. He wasn't all that sure he wanted to be saved. More than anything, Hunter wanted to strip off both their shirts and let the air at their overheated bodies.

"Hey, hey, what's this" came a voice. "Hunter, Hunter, Hunter...why, I guess we need to have a man-to-man talk, eh, my friend?"

Hunter reluctantly stepped back, holding Johanna's arms until she steadied herself.

"Charlie, what—"

Her younger brother held up a silencing hand. "Don't worry, Johanna, I'll handle this. Your friend here is a man and a real man not only doesn't eat quiche, he doesn't use."

Hunter never took his eyes off Johanna. "That's right."

"Which means he knows the feminine mind is going to interpret all this heavy-duty physical activity going on in here just now as more than just a physical attraction. Why, Johanna's female brain is probably flipping through her mental catalog of diamond ring styles even as we speak."

"I doubt she's gone quite that far, Charlie," Hunter said quietly.

"Yeah, well, according to you it won't be long before she is, so you'd better pull back and regroup real fast, man, if putting the moves on my sister doesn't mean anything to you."

"So when it's your own sister, suddenly it's not okay for a guy to use, Charlie?"

"It didn't mean anything to you?" Johanna asked, coming out of her daze in a hurry. Her voice sounded hurt.

"Your brother thinks he's got me between a rock and a hard place, Johanna, but he's wrong. I meant everything I said to him. Using a woman to scratch an itch is wrong and I'm not a user. When I make love, you can bet it means something to me. Meaningless sex is just that. This meant something, Johanna. I did not do it casually or without thinking first. Read between *those* lines, Charlie."

"Oh, my," said Johanna.

Chapter Seven

Hunter left both Johanna and Charlie in the kitchen with their mouths hanging open. He gathered up his foursome and took them home, knowing he'd be back on the morrow for another bout. He didn't know if he should celebrate or gird his loins. His life had become a mass of confusion that only a Hollywood scriptwriter would recognize.

"Maybe they'll get Tom Hanks to play my part," he muttered consolingly to himself after he'd finally wrestled the crew into bed and was tiptoeing out of the last bedroom. Him, a grown man, tiptoeing. "Ludicrous," he said. "Next thing you know I'll be offering to meet her at the top of the Empire State Building." He snorted. His girlfriend de jour when *Sleepless in Seattle* had come out had insisted on renting *An Affair to Remember,* he recalled. And when Cary Grant and Deborah Kerr had made arrangements to meet on the top of the Empire State Building, they'd given themselves a year, as he recalled, but as he thought about it, it might have been six months.

"Who cares," Hunter said, and shrugged. The point was, they'd given themselves a decent amount of time to get their lives straightened out before coming together again. Fat lot of good six months or even a year would do him. The way his life was rapidly spiraling downhill, he'd need half a century, at least.

"Oh well, maybe Johanna will take pity on me," he muttered as he applied his toothbrush vigorously to his teeth, too tired to stay up and enjoy the peace and quiet now that the children were down. He spit in the sink and inspected his handiwork in the mirror. He didn't think his face had aged too badly in the last month and a half, but feeling decidedly persecuted, Hunter shook his fist heavenward and swore, "I'll get you for this, Robert, see if I don't." Damn but he missed his brother. So did the kids. They'd had trouble falling asleep again tonight, but he'd managed to soothe and reassure them.

He lay in bed, full of self-pity and self-contradictions. He hadn't wanted to get married before he'd inherited Robert's children. He'd enjoyed the life of the footloose bachelor. Now that he'd decided he needed a mother for the unholy foursome and was willing to make the ultimate sacrifice at the marriage altar, Hunter found himself full of resentment. At first he'd shamelessly used the children to attract Johanna, knowing full well her love for the little ones. Now he found himself in the position where he didn't want to come through the back door to get her interest. Hunter wanted Johanna's interest to be focused on *him*.

He turned on his stomach and ruthlessly beat his pillow into shape underneath him.

"Go figure," he muttered as he concentrated hard on keeping his eyes shut. "Throw a drowning man a lifeline and he complains if the rope isn't brand-new."

Only no one had thrown him the lifeline just yet, certainly not Johanna, so how could he complain? First he had to get her, *then* he'd allow himself the luxury of complaining.

"Well, we'll just see about that," he told himself, eyes

popping back open in the darkened room despite his best effort. "Tomorrow she gets the double whammy. The kids first, then me. I'll pay Grace or Chris to watch the kids while I take her out to dinner tomorrow night. Someplace decent, not just any old place." He stayed awake long past midnight racking his brain, trying to come up with the exact right restaurant.

The sun rose long before Hunter was ready.

Mikie and Aaron rose shortly after the sun.

Aaron bounced on the end of the bed. Mikie, always one to try and outdo his brother regardless of the age difference, bounced directly on Hunter's back. Mikie peeled away the pillow Hunter had buried his head under. "Uncle Hunter!" he shouted right in Hunter's ear. "Wake up!"

Hunter groaned and prayed for a quick and merciful death. He'd be sure to report to Robert how Mikie's *r*'s had improved in the short amount of time Mikie had been with Hunter. Yes, he'd be sure to rub that in his brother's face once he joined him up in heaven.

"What is it, Mikie?" he asked in a barely discernible whisper. He was too tired from his restless night to work up enough energy to do anything more. He couldn't even work up enough strength to protest the abuse his back and eardrums were taking.

"It's morning, Uncle Hunter," Aaron pointed out help- fully in case the sunlight streaming directly over his face now that Mikie had tossed his pillow to the floor wasn't clue enough.

"Is the house on fire?" Hunter questioned.

"I don't think so," Aaron said. "Want I should go check?"

"No. I want you to go back to bed."

"But Aaron and me is hungry," Mikie complained. "We needs breakfast."

All right, so they'd have to work on matching subject to verb a bit. Hunter figured he ought to take care of that first.

then he'd go join his brother. "Probably sitting up there with a big bowl of corn chips and salsa," Hunter muttered as he rolled carefully to his side. He didn't want Mikie tumbling off the bed and hurting himself. "Watching some never-ending football game and pointing his finger this way and laughing at me during the commercial breaks." What in the world would they find to advertise in heaven? Wings with more lift? A broader wingspan? Polish specially formulated for halos? What?

Blearily, Hunter sat on the edge of the bed. "All right, what do you two want for breakfast? Make it simple," he warned. "I'm not up to crêpes suzette at this time of the morning."

"What's crêpe…what you said?"

"Something that's not on the menu. How about cereal with banana cut up in it?" Hunter asked. "Doesn't that sound good?"

"How 'bout pancakes?" countered Mikie.

"French toast," said Aaron.

Hunter groaned and stood. He ran a hand through his disheveled hair and grimaced. He wasn't at all sure he could handle staring at a bowl of raw eggs this early in the morning. "How about you two deciding on one thing? Let me know when I get out of the shower."

"Pancakes."

"French toast."

Hunter closed the bathroom door and turned the water on full blast in an effort to drown out the burgeoning breakfast argument. Six hours before he could drop them off with Johanna. Leaning his head against the shower stall wall, he let the water beat down on him. He could do this. It was all a question of willpower and staying power. He'd handled tougher clients than these four.

No, he hadn't.

Karen and Robby had awakened and found their way downstairs before Mikie and Aaron had reached consensus.

Two more voices added themselves to the confusion. Hunter held his head in one hand while he shoveled in cereal with the other. It had no discernible taste he could detect but it did promise an entire day's supply of vitamins. He figured he'd need them. He listened to the continued bickering while he chewed and swallowed.

If Johanna were here she'd know what to do.

Hell, if Johanna were here Hunter doubted he'd even notice the arguing. He'd be too busy staring at her and imagining her naked. Imagining his hands on all that beautiful nakedness. Imagining his mouth on... He groaned. Damn, but he was getting too old for this constant state of semiarousal.

Hunter picked up his bowl and rinsed the soggy flakes down the garbage disposal. "Everybody quiet down. Here's what's going to happen," he announced.

"Uncle Hunter—"

"I said quiet. We can't be doing this every morning. Nobody will ever get any breakfast. You'll all starve to death. I'll be arrested for child neglect. From now on we're going to take turns starting youngest to oldest. Mikie, what's for breakfast?"

"Pancakes," Mikie announced firmly. "I want pancakes and cut-up bananas," he added as a concession to his uncle's strange fruit fetish.

The kid might be temporarily the runt of the litter, but Hunter admired his tenacity. Mikie never gave an inch. "Fine. Pancakes it is."

"But I wanted French toast," Aaron wailed.

"Tomorrow is your turn, Aaron. This morning we're having pancakes. The alternative choice is Good Morning cereal. It's loaded with vitamins and fiber. End of discussion." Hunter reached into the pantry and retrieved the pancake mix. Aaron made a few more attempts to get his way, but Hunter ignored them, calmly mixing up the batter and drizzling it in neat puddles on the griddle he'd set up. They all ate. Hunter felt he'd turned some sort of corner that morning.

Buoyed by a successful breakfast Hunter experimented further. Rather than leaving the children to entertain themselves while he tried to accomplish any given task around the house, a recipe he'd already discovered led to bedlam and generalized destruction of some part of the house, Hunter assigned them each a small task. The instructions he gave with the task were geared to leave the impression that the fate of the free world rested on the job's successful completion.

Hunter's conclusion was that he was a damn marvel. Sir Isaac Newton, Louis Pasteur and Albert Einstein *combined* couldn't top him when he was on a roll.

"Mikie, your job is to pick up all the toy cars and put them in their basket on the shelf. I might step on one when I bring the clean clothes up, slip and fall, break my leg. Then I'd lose my job, wouldn't be able to pay the mortgage and we'll all have to go live in a cave."

Mikie looked sort of intrigued with the idea of living in a cave. Hunter realized he'd have to fine-tune his threats.

"Aaron, you're with me while I sort out the laundry from the dryer. You can help me fold and you'll have to tell me what belongs to whom. Otherwise my underwear might end up in your basket. If that happens they might fall down because they'll be so big on you. It will probably happen right in the middle of nursery school and all the girls will say *woo-ee* to you. And wouldn't it be a terrible thing if *Karen's* underwear ended up in your basket?" Hunter shuddered convincingly.

Aaron went pale and Hunter knew he was on the right track. Damn, but he was a genius.

"Robby, you're old enough to empty the dishwasher and put all the clean stuff away."

"I used to help my mom," Robby confirmed. "Sometimes I have to use a chair, but I'll be careful. Mom always said she didn't want my brains making a mess on her clean floor.''

"See? I knew you were big enough.'' Hunter beamed at his nephew. This was too easy. "Just last night I was noticing how big your biceps, uh, the muscles in your arms were getting, and I said to myself, why, that boy's big enough to empty the dishwasher.'' Hunter's expression turned serious. "Wouldn't it just be too bad if we ran out of clean dishes? We'd have to eat off the floor and some little boy I know spilled his orange juice this morning and didn't bother to wipe it up. I'd sure hate to eat off that floor right now, wouldn't you?''

"It's all sticky,'' Karen chipped in. "Your shoes squinch when you walk on it. His dinner would probably get stuck to the floor and he wouldn't get nothing to eat at all if that happened.'' She pointed at her chest. "We wouldn't, neither.''

"I noticed that very same thing, Karen, so know what you get to do?''

Karen shook her head. She had no clue.

"I'm going to get you a sponge mop and a bucket of soapy water. You're going to have a great time mopping the floor. Won't that be fun? And when it's done Coach Jo won't be in danger of having her shoe stick to it next time she comes over, falling over when she tries to walk because her shoe is stuck to the floor, breaking her leg and then not being able to coach swimming anymore because she'll be in traction with her leg in a cast in the hospital.''

Karen's eyes widened. "That would be bad.''

"Terrible,'' Hunter agreed, shaking his head mournfully.

"But if we didn't have to swim my hair won't turn green like Grace said it would.''

"I bought you the anti-chlorine shampoo.''

"And it might be fun to visit Coach Jo in the hospital. I could make her a card and you could get her flowers. I saw some at the grocery store. Pink and purple. They were pretty.''

"We're still going to wash the floor. If you slip and break your leg, you won't be able to go visit Coach Jo.''

"Oh, that's right.''

But it had been a mistake to bring Johanna into the conversation. The mere mention of her name had Hunter itching to get over there, to see her again, talk to her again.

Aaron was more in the way than a help in the laundry room, but at least Hunter knew where the child was. He handed him a size three boy's briefs and told him to put them in Robby's basket.

"Uncle Hunter, those are Robby's,'' Aaron explained on a sigh. "Robby can't wear those. He's too big. So am I.''

What kind of underwear did Johanna wear?

"Really? Silly me. Okay, put them in Mikie's basket so long as you're sure.''

Utilitarian cotton?

"I'm sure.''

Slinky silk?

"I'm glad you're helping me, Aaron. I'd be lost without you.''

High-cut panties or low-cut?

Hunter held up a pair of lace-edged little girl's panties. "Who do you suppose these belong to?''

How low-cut? Would Johanna wear lace?

"Those are Karen's,'' Aaron said, shaking his head sadly. He took them from his uncle and, tongue between his teeth as he concentrated, he carefully folded them into fourths and placed the panties in his sister's basket. "You're lucky we came to live with you, Uncle Hunter.''

"I know, Aaron. I'd be lost without your help.'' It would never occur to the little one that without him and his siblings there would be no laundry to sort. It would all be Hunter's. And it would certainly never occur to him that his uncle was pulling his leg and could distribute clothing very adequately without his guidance. But Aaron was right in one respect. After having them for almost two months now, Hunter would definitely miss them should the lot of them up and disappear. He'd be lonely.

It was with great relief that Hunter handed the last scrap of underwear to Aaron to fold and place in the appropriate laundry basket. "There," Hunter said with relief. "I'll get you a chair. You reach inside the washing machine and hand me the wet stuff. We'll get it all into the dryer, then start another load going in the washer. Darks this time, I guess. You can sort through the stuff on the floor and hand it to me so I don't make a mistake. If any of your white socks get in there by accident, they'll come out all yucky-looking."

"Really?" Aaron asked interestedly, a lightbulb obviously lighting inside his head. "I had a really cool pair of socks, only one of them got pink when Mommy washed them."

"There you have it," Hunter said. "It obviously snuck in with the colored clothes when Mom wasn't looking. They're sneaky like that. Gotta watch them every minute when you're doing the laundry."

Aaron eyed the floor suspiciously. "I'll watch 'em, Uncle Hunter."

"Good boy," said Hunter, and found he meant it.

They worked together in companionable silence for a short while. Hunter worked on shutting out thoughts of Johanna while they separated the remaining clothing. Aaron finally broke the quiet.

"Uncle Hunter?"

"Yeah?" Hunter straightened out a balled-up pair of navy blue shorts before dropping them into the washer.

"I really liked those socks."

"We'll go shopping some day soon," he promised. "See if we can find another pair."

"Uncle Hunter?"

He turned a red T-shirt right side out. "Yeah?"

"I miss my mommy." Aaron's voice quavered, and Hunter immediately panicked. He'd never been good at tears. Hell, he'd never been much good at any kind of emotions at all. He'd always figured it was a guy thing and hadn't worried overly much. Lately, unfortunately, Hunter had found himself positively bombarded with emotions and feelings. He was shell-shocked, that was the problem. Shell-shocked.

"I do, too," Hunter responded. It was the truth and devastating in its simplicity. He missed his sister-in-law and the way she'd always baked him an apple pie when he came to visit. Mary Ellen had had a way with crusts. She'd never figured out fried chicken, but her pie crusts more than made up for that flaw.

Hunter missed his brother punching him in the arm by way of greeting. He missed their wrestling matches and Mary Ellen's scolding and complaining about the extra two children in the house. He'd handled his grief by burying it in anger. He'd been just plain mad at his brother and his wife for doing this to him. How dare they up and die like this? But now it looked as though the children were finally realizing that their parents were not coming back. Hunter was doing his best to help them handle their grief and sense of desertion, but he felt inadequate to the task sometimes, as he was still struggling to handle his own feelings.

Damn it all, why'd they have to go and get themselves killed like that?

It wasn't fair, it just wasn't fair.

Hunter felt like a child himself railing against the injustices of life. He also felt just plain helpless. Not knowing what else to do, Hunter sank down onto the chair he'd brought in for Aaron's use and lifted the child onto his lap. Hunter snuggled Aaron up against his chest and rubbed the child's back while the little one shoved his face up against his neck and wept loud, gulping tears. Hunter's hearing would never be the same.

Neither would his heart. Aaron and his siblings were permanently imbedded in it now.

Finally the tears abated. Pulling his head back, Hunter tried to see Aaron's face and failed. "Feel better?" he asked.

Aaron rubbed his eyes with his fists and swiped at his nose with the back of his hand. "I guess. I just want them to come back now. They've been gone a long time."

Hunter sneaked a quick swipe at his own eyes. "They would if they could, buddy."

"Maybe if I'm extra special good?"

Oh, man. "No, Aaron, not even then. Mom and Dad didn't go away because you were bad or because they were mad at any of you guys. They didn't want to go away at all. Sometimes bad things just happen for no reason. They're in heaven where we can't see them right now, and they want us to stay here for now and for you and the rest of the guys to grow big and strong here with me." They'd covered this ground before. Hunter hoped it would eventually sink in.

Aaron, who Hunter knew had stopped sucking his thumb a year ago, laid his head against Hunter's chest and popped his thumb into his mouth. "Okay," the little boy finally quietly agreed. "You won't go away, will you, Uncle Hunter?"

"Not if there's any way to get around it, I won't. I promise, Aaron."

Aaron nodded his head and snuggled closer.

Hunter drove to Johanna's feeling as though he'd lanced a boil. After the scene in the laundry room with Aaron, he'd sat Karen and Robby down for yet another talk. Only this time, they seemed ready to listen. They, too, had evidently been wondering who'd been so bad that their parents had died. This morning they'd actually opened up to him. They'd both harbored a tremendous amount of guilt as they'd thought of every minor transgression they'd ever committed and hoped against hope the whole mess was somehow all the other guy's fault. Hunter wasn't so naive as to believe one good discussion would cure the problem, but he felt they'd finally started on the road to recovery. He'd do his damnedest to help. He felt good as he pulled into Johanna's driveway. Sort of like a drunk who'd been out reeling around in the dark and finally stumbled his way into an AA meeting.

Johanna met him at the door. Had she been watching for him?

"Hey," he said, grinning like a fool. Damn, but she looked good in her snug, worn jeans, sports sandals and loose T-shirt.

"Hi," Johanna said, smiling right back. She held the door open for them. "I wasn't quite sure exactly what time you'd be by."

Hunter checked his wristwatch. Five minutes to twelve. "You said lunch, right?"

Johanna nodded, still smiling. "Hi, guys, what's up? You hungry? Stephen and I have grilled cheeses ready to pop in the pan as soon as you got here."

"I'm starved," Robby confirmed. "I had to empty the dishwasher."

"Oh yeah?" Karen interjected. "Well I had to wash the floor so Coach Jo wouldn't stick to it and hurt herself, so I'm *super-duper* hungry."

"Oh, yeah? Well—"

Maybe he shouldn't have tried to alleviate *all* the guilt. A little bit of guilt could be a good thing, at least in securing good behavior. Hunter shook his head. No, this was healthier. Damn it.

The kids argued their way into the kitchen, leaving Johanna and Hunter staring at each other.

"Sounds like you had a busy morning. Is the floor worse or better than when she started? How many dishes have you got left?"

"Hey, they did good work. Take after their uncle." He leaned forward and kissed Johanna's mouth. "Hi again," Hunter said softly.

Johanna returned the favor, kissing him right back. "Hello, yourself."

"Damn, but you smell good."

Johanna blushed. "I, um, just cleaned one of the bathrooms. There's a hint of lemon in the cleaner I used."

"You'll have to give me its name," Hunter murmured, lowering his mouth once more.

"Hey, Jo, we got a chip limit or what?" Stephen yelled from the kitchen.

"Chip limit?" Hunter questioned.

Johanna broke eye contact. "Yes," she called back. "Five chips, four baby carrots, three apple slices and two sandwich triangles. Count them with Mikie, will you? They can have more chips if they clean their plates of that much."

"You mean we gotta use plates?"

"Yes, plates. The plastic ones."

"You're washing 'em."

"Fine. I'll take care of the dirty dishes, but we're civilized here and do not eat directly off the tabletop."

Stephen snorted. You could hear it two rooms away. "That's what you think."

Johanna sighed. "I better get in there. Do you want to say goodbye or did you do that in the car?"

With Johanna smiling up at him, Hunter was having difficulty remembering what had been so all-fired important to get done that he needed to leave at all. He scratched his head while he thought. "I think I probably threatened them sufficiently in the car," he admitted. "Still, one more time can't hurt." He followed Johanna out to the kitchen.

Stephen glanced up as they came into the room. "We coulda used napkins instead of plates, you know," he said. "You can throw those out when you're done."

"I said I'd wash the dirty dishes, Stephen," Johanna reminded him. "Thanks for making the sandwiches."

"Yeah, well, okay."

"Tell Grace I said she was to go check on Mom."

"What do I get if I do?"

"You need to worry about what you'll get if you don't." Stephen left.

Hunter eyed his crew sternly. "All right, you guys, I'm going to the hardware store to get the screws I need for Karen's shelves and do a few other errands. I don't want any bad reports when I get back."

"We know, we know. You're gonna hang us out with the wash if we give Coach Jo any trouble," Robby said, and rolled his eyes skyward. For a little kid, he was already pretty good at that.

"That's right, so behave, all of you."

"You'll come back, right, Uncle Hunter?"

"I promise, Aaron, I'll be back." Hunter took off his wristwatch and handed it to the little tyke. "Look here. When this little hand gets down here to the six and this big one is pointing straight up, I'll be back."

"How will you know what time it is if you give Mikie your watch?" questioned Karen.

"Yeah, besides, I want it instead of him," said Robby.

Hunter just sighed, shook his head and left, but one of the first stops he made was at a discount store. He bought them all cheesy inexpensive action figure watches with the realization he was going to have to be scrupulously careful getting back on time whenever he left them now, at least for the next little while.

Hunter went to the grocery store and zipped through the place. There was a brief debate between baked chicken or pot roast for tomorrow's supper. Hunter held one in each hand and wondered which Johanna preferred, then realized he was being silly. She wouldn't be there for Sunday dinner. As an added benefit, his bill was half the normal one when the kids were with him asking for every other item on the shelf.

He stopped at a fast-food place for a late lunch and ate a giant fries, bacon and cheese on his burger, and had a shake for his drink. Then Hunter ordered a sundae with Spanish peanuts and extra whipped cream for dessert. He was by himself and relished not having to set a good example for anybody. The only problem was, Hunter wished there'd been somebody, preferably Johanna, there with him to share the wickedness of the moment.

Leaving the burger place, Hunter drove home and assembled Karen's shelves. Forty-five minutes later he stepped back to admire the shelves and found himself wishing Johanna was there to impress with his handiwork.

This was ridiculous. He'd always been a loner, quite content to spend most of his time by himself, and suddenly he couldn't handle a couple of hours on his own? Man, he was really slipping.

So what did he do? Hunter went downstairs to check that the bouquet of fresh flowers he'd picked up at the grocery store had all its stems deep enough into the cup of water he'd stuck them in to actually get a drink. Johanna wouldn't be impressed by a bunch of drooping, sagging, sad-looking things, now would she?

"Oh, you've got it bad," Hunter told himself as he took one of his good steak knives and freshened the cuts on the bottoms of the stems so the flowers could suck up more water. He'd read that somewhere. "Wonder if I've got any aspirin?" Hunter asked in a one-way conversation with himself. "Didn't I read that crushing one up in the flower water did something or another for them?" Leaving the kitchen for the bathroom, Hunter searched the medicine cabinet and actually found a jar. His hand hesitated, hovering over the job. "Or was that heart attack victims you were supposed to give it to? Shoot, I don't remember. Still, what can a little pain reliever hurt?" He took the jar back to the kitchen, crushed one up and threw it in, then glanced at the clock.

He'd wasted an entire forty-five minutes of his free time preventing any headaches from popping up in a bunch of daisies. "You are really losing it," he told himself.

Determinedly, he went out to the garage to clean out and vacuum his car. He had to pick up a couple of corporate bigwigs at the airport Monday morning. He'd still done nothing about replacing the vehicle for one with more safety belts. Briefly he entertained himself with thoughts of car shopping. "Johanna likes blue. I wonder if that preference extends to minivans," he said out loud. "Oh, stop, would you please?" Hunter ordered himself when he realized what he'd just said. "Just stop."

Finally, finally, finally, it was time to go back to the Durbins' and pick up his brood. And Johanna, let's not forget Johanna, Hunter reminded himself, which was a ridiculous worry since she'd cropped up in every other thought he'd had all day. He was hardly likely to forget her at this point in the day.

"Still, that's okay," he told himself. "It still isn't ninety-seven percent of the time. If I get up over ninety percent, I'll start worrying. Then I'll know I'm obsessing like Charlie, but I'm still okay where I am now."

Sure he was.

Chapter Eight

Hunter had to turn around and go back for the flowers he'd left in their cup in his sink, but he'd allowed extra time, so other than the stain from the water on his car seat, it wasn't a problem. He rang Johanna's doorbell promptly at 6:00 p.m. by his car clock.

"Hi," he said when Johanna opened the door. He couldn't help but grin even while he cringed a bit inside. He probably looked like an idiot standing there smiling stupidly with a bunch of dripping flowers.

Johanna felt all hot and flustered compared to the way Hunter looked. She'd chased kids around all day, and the dust bunnies she'd dueled with under Stephen and Will's beds had been no cute baby bunnies. They'd been big enough to grow fangs and star in a horror movie. The Dust Bunny that Ate the World. She'd bravely vanquished them but was definitely suffering from battle fatigue.

Not Hunter, though, Johanna thought, smiling in return to his infectious grin. Had he taken the afternoon to sleep in? What had happened to his list of jobs he'd wanted to get done? Hunter looked disgustingly energetic and, well, darn sexy. It hardly seemed fair for him to be radiating with health and sex appeal while Johanna stood there feeling like a limp, wet rag.

Johanna gathered her shoulder-length blond hair into both hands and held it up so air could get at her hot neck and hopefully cool it off a bit. "Come on in," she said, and was proud when she remembered to step back so he could.

"Kids good?" Hunter asked as he stepped over the threshold.

Johanna waved away any concerns. "Oh, sure. Few little squabbles, nothing major."

Hunter's eyes narrowed suspiciously. He loved his niece and nephews dearly, but he was their parent now, no longer an uncle who could afford to spoil them, then send them home to get straightened out. *He* was home. And he didn't like the idea of anyone, not even half pints like his own crew, giving Johanna a hard time.

"If they were all that good why are you so hassled-looking?" he asked bluntly.

Johanna flushed with embarrassment. She must really look terrible for Hunter to forget his manners enough to mention it. Heck, even that second night when Aaron and Mikie had fallen into the swimming pool and half drowned, Hunter had been unfailingly polite. Self-consciously, she tucked her hair behind her ears. "Will's allergies have been acting up. Mom, Charlie and I launched a major cleaning campaign in the room he shares with Stephen, then we made a stab at the main living areas. Mom's not feeling too well so's she's lying down now but Will should sleep better tonight." Johanna gestured at Hunter's clean, crisp navy slacks and gray knit polo-style shirt. "What's your excuse for looking so spiffy? How come you aren't all hot and sweaty-looking? Just look at you. You're gorgeous."

And he was. His shirt, with its three narrow navy pinstripes of color that streaked horizontally across it, seemed specially made to show off his broad chest. It wasn't fair. It just wasn't fair.

The disgusted look Johanna gave Hunter had him wondering if it was a compliment or not. Did she really think he was good-looking? He'd always dressed for success, not to impress women. They'd been sort of a side benefit. The strategy was paying off in the corporate world. Wouldn't it be nice if it paid off in his personal life as well? He was glad he'd taken the time to shower and shave, even if it meant staying up late tonight to finish the last few jobs he'd had scheduled for the day. Getting Johanna to notice him as a man was worth it.

Johanna continued. "You don't have a hair out of place. What did you decide to do, take the afternoon off instead of working?"

Still, Hunter was compelled to defend himself. He didn't want Johanna thinking he was useless. "Actually, I got quite a bit of work done. I just cleaned up a bit before I came over. I was hoping to talk you into letting me take you out for dinner. I thought maybe Grace could baby-sit for the gang. She must be saving up for something. Kids always are. And I pay well." Then he shoved the dripping flowers at her. "Here, these are for you."

Johanna felt really dumb then. She should have been watching the clock. She should have cleaned herself up a bit before Hunter had returned. Darn it, she didn't know anything about attracting a man. She'd never had the time to worry about things like that before. She was taking the time now. Johanna accepted the flowers in shock. "You want to take me out to dinner?"

Hunter studied her face. Why did she look and sound so puzzled? Surely she'd been asked out before. "Yeah, that was the general idea. I've got reservations for seven-thirty, just in case you agreed."

Johanna worried her bottom lip with her teeth. Seven-thirty? She pushed a lock of hair that had fallen forward back behind her ear again. It would take every bit of that time just to make herself marginally presentable. "To a real restaurant with food I didn't have to make myself?"

Hunter laughed, turned her around and shooed her toward the staircase with a friendly swat on her backside. "I can see the idea appeals. Go on, get ready. Where are the kids? I figured Aaron would be hanging out the front window watching for me."

"I just checked on them. They're all involved in a highly competitive game of Chutes and Ladders right now. Will almost won, but then he landed on the square with that long, long chute and he's practically back at the beginning now while Karen just took a ladder up two levels. She's currently heading the pack." She gestured toward the back of the house. "They're in the family room. Go on back while I jump in the shower."

Instead of moving, Hunter stood at the bottom of the stairs and watched the sway of Johanna's hips as she hurried up the stairs. Probably she'd put on old jeans that had shrunk from too many washings and a T-shirt that had met the same fate to save her good clothes while she cleaned, but watching that snuggly encased little rear of hers swing as she took the steps, well, if anyone ever thought to sell tickets, Hunter would be first in line to pay the price of admission. He took a deep breath and blew it out. "Down boy," he ordered.

Johanna had reached the landing. She half turned, looking down. "What's the matter?"

"Nothing," Hunter lied. His voice hadn't switched octaves on him in fifteen years, yet he was oddly grateful to hear his normal low tone when he spoke. He held up his hands. "Drop the flowers down to me. I'll put them in the kitchen."

"No way. They'll get wrecked throwing them around like that. I'm keeping them with me."

Hunter shrugged. "Okay." But he still didn't move.

"The family room's back down the hall." Johanna pointed the way with her hand.

"Yeah, I know."

She arched a questioning brow when he still didn't move. "Well?"

"Uh, nothing." Hunter cleared his throat. "Nothing at all. On my way." He gestured down the hallway himself. "That way, right?"

Nodding, Johanna agreed, "Uh-huh."

"Right. I'm going. See me go." And he greatly feared he was gone. Over Johanna.

Johanna gave him an odd look, then continued up the stairs.

"Uncle Hunter!" Aaron called out as soon as he saw Hunter. "You're back already?"

Hunter glanced at his wrist as he'd done any number of other times that afternoon from force of habit. It was blank. "Half past a freckle," he muttered to himself as he remembered an old childhood joke. He searched the room, finally settling on a digital readout displayed on the VCR that resided on a shelf just below the TV in an inexpensive wood-toned entertainment unit. It was six-thirteen.

"I said six o'clock, didn't I?"

Aaron pulled on his shirtfront. Hunter noticed there was a string pinned to it. As Aaron pulled on the string, Hunter's watch came into view, dangling from the string's end. Aaron studied the face of the watch. The watch would have been too large for Aaron's wrist, of course. Johanna must have worried the little one would lose it and had taken the time to employ countermeasures. The woman knew children and had a wide streak of thoughtfulness that still caught Hunter by surprise.

"The little hand is on the six, but the big hand isn't straight up," he finally reported quite seriously.

Hunter had arrived on time according to the car clock, but had dawdled in the front hall with Johanna for several minutes, thirteen to be exact if the digital readout on the family room's VCR unit was set correctly. He wasn't going to be the one to point the lapsed deadline out to Aaron. Not knowing what to say, Hunter settled on "Okay." He turned to Grace, where she was reading a book in the corner of the L-shaped sectional sofa. "Grace, you want to earn some money tonight?"

No dummy, Grace quickly questioned the amount. "How much?"

Clueless as to the going rate, Hunter responded with a questioning, "Five bucks an hour?"

"Doing what?"

"Baby-sitting the crew while I take your sister out for dinner."

"You'll pay me? Real money?"

Sensing her weakness, Hunter quickly assured her, "Of course real money. What other kind is there?"

"I didn't get paid for this afternoon," Grace pointed out logically, "'cuz family chips in. I either had to help clean Will's room or keep my eye on the shrimpsters down here. No way was I going to touch anything in Will's room."

Hunter cleared his throat manfully. He remembered the typical condition of his own room at Will's age. Next year's science experiments were probably already well under way on every available surface up there. "Can't say I blame you, but I promise I'm really going to pay you. Cold, hard cash." He slipped out his wallet and searched out a twenty. He held it up to demonstrate.

Grace eyed it. The look in her eyes told Hunter she wanted it. He suspected it was her family position, coming in after the two boys, that had her behaving so suspiciously.

"Why do they call money cold or hard?"

Hunter waved it a bit right under her nose. "I have no idea. Yes or no?"

"Hey, what's this?" Chris asked as he came into the room. "Twenty bucks? What for?"

Grace snatched the twenty and stuffed it in her pocket. "For me. It's for me 'cuz I'm gonna baby-sit Hunter's kids tonight."

Chris glanced calculatingly at the small fry surrounding the game board. "Make it twenty-five and I'll do it. I'm older."

"You can't," Grace flung back. "He already asked me. Didn't you, Hunter?"

"Yes, I did. I wanted somebody who'll actually play with them and read them a bedtime story. I don't want them just put in front of a TV while the sitter yaks on the phone all night."

"That's asking a lot, man," Chris warned. "Thirty bucks."

"I'm happy with the deal I've got," Hunter said, and smiled at Grace. In eighth grade, she was in the midst of a growth spurt. All arms, legs and sharp angles, Grace was on the verge of blooming into a beauty. Given a few years, she would be a darker-haired version of Johanna.

Grace grinned back. Hunter surmised she didn't come out on top in a competition with her older sibling all that frequently and felt doubly good about his choice.

He sank down onto the old family room sofa and began indiscriminately teasing his own four along with Johanna's younger siblings. When she arrived downstairs forty-some minutes later, Johanna walked into a wrestling match. Hunter was on the bottom of the pile.

"This is why Mom has never replaced the furniture in here," she said as the lamp next to the sofa wobbled dangerously. "You guys know you're not supposed to roughhouse in here."

"He started it."

Six young voices yelled the accusation simultaneously. Johanna sighed and shook her head. There was little doubt in her mind to whom the "he" referred.

Robby glanced up from his position straddling Hunter's

chest. The child stared. "Wow, Coach Jo, you sure look different."

Still clinging tenaciously to Hunter's leg, Will commented, "Hey, Jo, I didn't know you had any skirts."

Aubrey felt obliged to defend her sister. "'Course she does, dummy. She's a girl, isn't she?"

"So are you and you don't have any skirts. Look at her. She's got nylons on and everything."

"We wore dresses on Easter," Grace contributed. "And I got to wear panty hose. Jo and Mom both said I was old enough. I shaved my legs and everything."

"You shaved your legs?" Karen asked. "With like a real razor like Uncle Hunter uses?" She turned to Johanna when Grace nodded. "Wow. Did you shave your legs for tonight, Coach Jo? Can I see? Can I feel? Are they real smooth now? Will you teach me how to do it?"

Hunter shook his arms free of Aaron and Karen, then lifted Mikie off his face. He raised his head to get a look at Johanna. His eyes widened. No wonder the kids were all fascinated. It was only natural for Karen to want to see and feel. He wanted to see and feel, too. Damn, but there were too many people around for his purposes. And there would be more than just Johanna and him in the restaurant later on. It had never concerned him before, but with his house full and Johanna's house full, where did you go to be alone with a good-looking woman when you lived in a city? Hunter supposed he could ask Charlie where the hot parking spots were, but man—

Still partially stunned from Johanna's transformation from merely beautiful to absolutely stunning, Hunter didn't react quickly enough when Karen grabbed his arm and effortlessly pushed it back down to the floor.

"Got you now, Uncle Hunter," the child crowed.

"Yeah, got you now!" Aaron yelled as he sprawled full body on the opposite appendage.

Got you now's echoed around the room. Mikie clambered back over his face. He'd been holding his own against the seven of them, but right then Hunter was a whipped man. He'd have trouble taking on a kitten at the moment. Then Johanna delivered the coup de grace.

"No, *I've* got *you* now," she said.

And Johanna repeated it as she plucked one child after another off his prone body. She was speaking to the children, Hunter knew, but he was the one who took it to heart, for he recognized its truth. She had him now. What he'd first thought of as almost a business deal had become a matter of the heart.

And those were always sticky.

Weren't they?

The date got off to a poor start, as Hunter didn't have enough safety belts to transport everyone back to his house.

"I'll drive as far as your place and bring Grace with me," Johanna told him practically. "That way you won't have to go back out again once dinner's over. I can take Grace home with me."

He wanted to argue. He wanted Johanna next to him starting right that minute. It wasn't that Hunter was into instant gratification or anything, he'd delayed being with her all afternoon, hadn't he? Listen to yourself, Hunter thought as he buckled children into safety belts. You're being pathetic.

Oh, yeah? Well too damn bad. Tomorrow—no tomorrow was Sunday and car dealers weren't open on Sundays— Monday then, *early* Monday he was going car shopping and buying himself the monster van from hell. One of those elongated jobs with twelve, fifteen safety belts. That way he'd never run out and this would never come up again. Not even if Johanna invited the entire swim team along for the ride.

Hunter scowled for the entire trip back to his house. He continued to scowl until he had Johanna right where he wanted her, which was seated next to him in a car empty but for the two of them.

"I didn't think we'd ever get them settled in," he told her.

"Kids have internal radar," Johanna informed Hunter. "They know sometimes even before you do what you want and then they do their utmost to frustrate you and keep you from getting it. It's some kind of gene for perversity that shuts down around twenty-one, though not always. Some people have a defective switch and they stay annoying their whole lives. I'm beginning to think Charlie may be one of those."

Hunter laughed. "Charlie's going to be okay." Hunter would personally see to it. Hunter began to edge the conversation in the way he wanted it to go. "So, you've been studying hard for your finals?"

Johanna rubbed her forehead. "Not as much as I'd have liked. There's been a little problem at home I've been trying to work out." Johanna gazed out the window as Hunter pulled into the restaurant's parking lot. Crowded tonight.

A problem besides the older boys? How many problems could one household have? Hunter frowned to himself. This wasn't the way this was supposed to go. Johanna had obviously not read the script Hunter had been scrolling through his mind when he'd planned his strategy earlier on. The woman was supposed to say yes, then Hunter had planned to make a comment or two about graduation, which would have led into a question on the résumés she'd sent out and her apartment hunt, to which she would hopefully have given a negative response. All of the above would have culminated with Hunter offering sympathy, then his far superior, alternative solution of marriage to him and the accompanying gratifying and fulfilling motherhood of Hunter's sterling charges such an honor would bestow on Johanna.

Unfortunately the woman couldn't follow a script for beans.

Hadn't he already taken care of Charlie's and Chris's sex life for her? A sex life evidently far more active than his own, he might add. She had more problems? Now what? Oh, for crying out loud.

Hunter pulled into a vacant spot, got out and circled around the car. He took a deep breath. Okay, all right, good things never came easily. You appreciated them more when you had to work for them, blah, blah, blah. And anyway, how big a problem could it be? Johanna's family was the very definition of wholesomeness. Surely this was a minor detour, a dip in the road, nothing more. So he'd pry the problem out of her, help her find the solution, *then* it was back to the script he'd written. With a vengeance. He really couldn't wait that much longer to get his hands on Johanna. It was requiring superhuman willpower as it was. Look at him, he'd actually left his niece and nephews with a babysitter for the first time since he'd gotten them. Hunter shook his head at the irony of it. The initial attraction had been her appeal as a mother for his brood, and the first opportunity he gets, what does he do? Kidnap the woman for an evening alone. Go figure.

Hunter opened Johanna's car door and escorted her into the restaurant, a hand on the small of her back guiding her. She felt good under his hand. Firm, supple. *Oh, just stop it, do you hear? Just stop it.* Hunter sighed right along with the restaurant door as it closed behind them. He held his own council while they waited for their table, making small talk, solving most of the world's problems during that twenty minutes, just not Johanna's. He even waited while she perused the menu, then again while the waiter wrote their selections down on his order pad. Their half carafe of wine came, the waiter pouring them each a glass of zinfandel. Finally, finally, he thought, the time was right to turn the conversation to something important.

"You mentioned a problem at home?"

Johanna glanced up from the roll she was mutilating. "Yeah. It's kind of on my mind all the time. I'm staring at my books but I'm thinking about this other thing instead of concentrating on what's right under my nose."

Hunter nodded in what he hoped was an understanding fashion. "I know how that can be. Rough. Maybe if you shared the problem with me, between the two of us we might be able to come up with a solution."

Johanna shook her head. "I don't think there is a solution to this one. At least not in the short term. It'll right itself in about twenty years or so."

"Now you've got my curiosity peaked. Come on, tell me."

"It's kind of personal," Johanna insisted, and gave a strained smile to the waiter when he slid a plate of salad in front of her. She picked up her fork and toyed with the torn lettuce. "And I know how protective you are of your niece and nephews. You might not want them coming around anymore."

Hunter reached across the table and captured her hand to hold it still. It was making him crazy and the conversation was starting to worry him. "I won't think less of you," he promised. "You'll feel better if you talk about it."

Staring into Hunter's eyes was like looking into a kaleidoscope done in shades of blue. Beautiful complicated patterns repeated themselves around the fathomless black pupils. It was easy to believe the secrets to the universe could be found in there. And he was right about one thing. If Johanna didn't talk to somebody about this pretty soon, she would go crazy.

"My mother's pregnant."

The bald statement hung in the air between them. Hunter's eyes shot wide open and he sat back in his chair. "What?" Surely he'd misheard.

Johanna leaned forward. She wasn't about to let anyone

overhear this particular conversation. "See, it all started when I found this pregnancy test kit in the trash." Johanna went on to relate the revelations of the past few days.

Hunter was just plain stunned. There was no other word for it. "But how did this happen?"

"The very thing I said." Johanna jumped on his question with an index finger poking the air between them as she emphasized her point. "You know what she said?"

"No, what?"

"She said it had happened in the usual way. Isn't that ridiculous?"

"That's not what you meant. You meant—"

"I know what I meant. So did she. She was just being difficult. Finally, last night after you went home?"

"Yeah?" If they leaned any farther over the tabletop Hunter would be in danger of setting his necktie on fire in the candle flame. He tucked the ends into the space between two buttons on his shirtfront.

"Finally, I got her to sit down and talk to me about it. She's been into avoidance, you know? And that doesn't work too well when you're talking pregnancy."

"No, I don't imagine it does." Frustrated with the width of the narrow table, Hunter got up and moved his chair to a position adjacent to Johanna's. He slid his right arm around Johanna's back and reached across his body with his left arm to intertwine fingers with her. She needed comforting and he needed the physical contact. "So anyway, you sat down with her last night after I left and she said what?"

Johanna leaned into Hunter's shoulder, grateful for his strength. "Mom reminded me of a business trip she'd taken six weeks ago."

"Obviously more than business took place."

"I have a lot of trouble thinking of my mother this way. It's weird. She's always been such a rock, you know? But you know what she said?"

Hunter fortified himself with a gulp of wine. "What?"

Johanna guzzled a bit of her own wine. She was still in shock. "Okay, I guess I'd better start at the beginning."

"Good thinking."

"Yes, well." Johanna paused to swipe a few wispy hairs back off her forehead. "She goes on this business trip to Washington."

"D.C. or state of? Never mind, I guess it doesn't matter."

"Actually it does. D.C. My mother loves museums. She used to drag us into Chicago all the time. I practically grew up in the Field Museum and Museum of Science and Industry. We couldn't afford to buy the food there so we'd bring a picnic and eat off the tailgate out in the parking lot before we went in. I remember one time…never mind, I'm getting sidetracked."

"So she's in D.C.," Hunter reminded her while he chewed a mouthful of wet salad. It didn't matter that it was soggy. He wasn't really tasting it, anyway.

"Right. Mom checks into the hotel and she's in the elevator going up to her room. It's late Sunday afternoon. The elevator's crowded, a lot of business people checking in for Monday morning meetings and things."

"Yeah? And?"

"Like I said, it's crowded so there are people close to her on all sides. They've all got luggage, too. This one guy has a carryall with a shoulder strap so his bag is up high practically right under Mom's nose, she said. Guess where the identification tag says he's from?"

"Elkhart, Indiana."

"Goshen."

"Close enough."

"Exactly. Here they meet a million miles away from home and it turns out their backyards practically back up to each other's. Naturally, she says something."

"Naturally. Truth be told, I grew up in Goshen. I'd have

struck up a conversation myself. Checked for mutual acquaintances, that kind of thing.''

"See? It's totally understandable. Later on when she goes down to eat dinner, who's down there?''

You didn't need a Ph.D. to answer that one. "The elevator man from Goshen.''

"Yes! They're both alone, his name gets called first, so what does he do?''

Hunter pushed his empty salad plate away. You had to admire this unknown guy's moves. "He offers to share his table with her. They talk. After dinner they go into the bar for a drink. There's a piano player so he asks her to dance. Then another drink.''

Johanna looked at Hunter admiringly. "How'd you know?''

Hunter shrugged modestly. "Lucky guess.'' Damn pervert, coming on to the mother of seven.

"You hit the nail right on the head. Remember I told you my mom loved museums?''

Hunter nodded. "You going to eat your salad?''

Johanna shoved the plate over. "No, you go ahead.''

Hunter picked up his fork. Listening to this unknown male's smooth moves and evident luck with those moves had him ravenous. Food would do for now. "Your mom loves museums and there she is in D.C. Her and the Smithsonian. There, together. I bet Goshen man offers to take her so she doesn't have to go all by her lonesome.''

Johanna looked at him admiringly. "You're amazing.''

Not as amazing as he intended to be, given half a chance. "And from there, things just…happened.'' Hunter nodded to himself. From the Smithsonian to bed, it was totally logical…to somebody, actually two somebodies. "I don't mean to be rude, but at her age, and with her concern over the boys, your mother never thought about birth control?''

Johanna squirmed in her chair. She shouldn't be discussing this with Hunter. It was family business. On the other hand, she really, really needed to talk about it with somebody. Of all her friends, even people she'd known years longer, it was Hunter's integrity she trusted most. What was spoken in confidence would remain in confidence. And it was Hunter's advice she'd find most valuable. "My mother hasn't had to worry about things like that, at least not in terms of herself, since my father died. Even then, my dad loved kids. They weren't concerned all that much with preventing babies. My mom was always involved in a loving relationship where it just didn't matter. She's just not used to thinking like that. She's actually very intelligent in most things, but she did say she thinks she was sort of temporarily off balance, tired of being alone, of being lonely."

The waiter appeared by the table laden with steaming plates of food. They both sat back while he delivered their dinners.

"Have a care," he advised. "Plates are hot."

"We'll watch it. Thank you," Hunter said, acknowledging the warning. He waited only long enough for the waiter to be out of hearing range. "How can anybody be lonely in a house with eight people living in it?" he asked.

"That's what I wanted to know. She said it's quite possible to be alone in a room full of people, and to tell you the truth, I understand exactly what she means."

Hunter paused with a morsel of steak halfway to his mouth. "You do?"

"Dad was Mom's high school sweetheart. They got married the summer after they graduated. Mom was eighteen when she had me. Once they realized how hard it was going to be to support a family Mom got a full-time job and started night classes while Dad went to college classes full-time and worked nights. He stuck with it until he had his MBA. That's why there's such a gap between Charlie and me."

"Ah."

"Anyway, my family position is kind of weird. Not a parent, except for kind of now, and not really a kid. It is lonely. I guess Mom's been feeling the lack of someone her own age even more."

Hunter swallowed and took more wine. "Okay, I guess I can understand that," he allowed, and he did. He himself now had a houseful of five, but after only a few months found himself longing for some adult companionship. Yes indeed, a partner with whom he could weather his current insanity would really be nice. Someone stable, there day in and day out so they'd know the background when he needed to think out solutions to the myriad problems the kids came up with. Still... "But what about the guy? What was his excuse?"

"His wife left him a few months ago. Came home from a business trip and the locks on the house had all been changed."

"Rough."

"He's a CEO or something, travels a lot. I guess she liked the position, status, house, et cetera the salary bought just fine, but issued an ultimatum to stop traveling or else. I got the impression the guy was still in shock, rather off balance himself, just like Mom."

Hunter sat back and thought about everything he'd heard. This situation was not going to be solved by taking the parties involved for a walk and a lecture. No, this mess was going to take a whole lot more to set it to rights, assuming that was even possible, than Charlie and Chris's fascination with the female form.

"Don't you see?"

"Don't I see what?" asked Hunter.

"I feel totally selfish. I mean, I should be focused on Mom, but all I can think about is that I'm not going to be able to move out in another month or two the way I'd planned. Somebody's going to have to be there for her. She's forty-three, for heaven's sake. This is going to be hard on her. And who's going to take care of the baby when it comes?" Johanna held up her hand in a stopping gesture when it looked as though Hunter was going to say something. "I'll tell you who. Me. I'll be living at home, taking care of siblings forever. And you want to know something?"

"What?" he asked cautiously, not liking the look of fire in her eye.

"That makes me darn mad. And being angry makes me feel guilty. Instead of putting my mother first, I'm spending all my time and energy feeling sorry for myself. How's that for self-centered?"

No, Hunter thought, this was not how he'd imagined the evening going. Not at all. And guess what? He was feeling damned angry himself and not just a little bit sorry for himself. Hunter sighed and massaged his temples. He prided himself on trying to foresee all possibilities. It was why he was so good in the business world. He refused to feel badly for not foreseeing this twist, however. Who the heck could have? Hell's bells, if he'd read it in a book he'd have thrown the book down in disgust and written a letter to the publisher asking for a more credible plotline next time. Which meant, of course, when one stopped to think about it, that Hunter **was** living a life too strange for fiction.

Well, damn.

Chapter Nine

Hunter spooned a major chunk of sour cream onto his baked potato and several pats of butter. Real butter. To hell with cholesterol. What was a clogged artery or two compared with everything else he had on his plate currently?

Halfway through the potato, he finally spoke. "I have to think about this."

"It won't help," Johanna informed him darkly. "God knows I've done nothing else but think about it since the moment I found out. I've thought so hard my brain is in serious danger of circuit meltdown. It's disorienting when you have to recognize that your parents are human and have failings and needs. They're supposed to be Rock of Gibraltar look-alikes, weather any storm kind of thing without showing any weathering in the process, you know? But the facts are, my mother is forty-three and pregnant. She has no partner. It falls to me as the oldest daughter to see her through this fiasco. It's some kind of unwritten societal law. There is no other solution. I'm doomed."

"Shh, I'm thinking."

"Yeah, well let me know if you come up with any sca-thingly brilliant ideas."

"You'll be the first," Hunter assured her. His dinner had lost its taste, but he cleaned his plate, anyway. Something told him he'd need the strength to see him through this latest fiasco. "Want any dessert?" he asked.

As a matter of fact, she did. Johanna felt the need of comfort food. A double fudge brownie sundae with extra whipped cream and nuts just might help.

It sounded good to Hunter. He had the same.

Shortly after, Johanna sat in the front seat of Hunter's car feeling slightly ill. "I shouldn't have eaten that whole thing," she admitted.

"Me neither," Hunter agreed. "Maybe we should try to walk it off." The restaurant he'd chosen was in South Bend, not too far from the East Race, a man-made diversion of the St. Joseph River that ran through the heart of down-town South Bend and was used for professional and ama-teur kayak events as well as for the more mundane rubber rafting. The park district had installed picturesque walk-ways along its edge. Hunter found a parking spot not too far from its starting gate.

"Come on," he said, taking her arm after opening her car door. "Let's work some of that dessert off."

They worked their way down to the waterway and found themselves one of many couples walking its length. Other couples who were very self-involved. Several were holding hands, most had gone further. *His* arm would be draped around *her* shoulder. *Her* arm was wrapped around *his* waist. One couple had their hands tucked into each other's back pockets. Hunter took in the scene. Glancing up he recognized the cloudless starlit skies. A full moon beamed down, making even the sparsely spaced streetlights super-fluous. A gentle breeze wafted over them, smelling exactly like the late-spring evening it was, with just a hint of the summer to come. In short, it was a night made for romance. The evening absolutely reeked of atmosphere.

Heck, why fight city hall?

Intending to take Johanna's hand in his, Hunter found himself putting an arm around her shoulders and tugging her gently closer instead. When Johanna responded by leaning her head against his shoulder and wrapping her own arm around his waist, he leaned down and kissed her. It was brief and closemouthed but he felt the resultant tremor right down to his size twelve feet.

There had to be a way out of this mess. There had to be.

"Johanna?"

"Hmm?"

"Did your mother mention a name at all?"

Johanna snorted delicately. "Smith, can you believe it? Jim Smith."

"Smith became trite *because* it was such a common name. *Somebody's* got to be named it for real." Although he doubted it in this case. Still, he needed to leave the door open a crack for himself as much as Johanna. He needed that ray of hope. The guy could still show up at some point. Right.

"I went to school with several of them. Jeremiah Smith was the center on the high school basketball team. And, um, I think there was a David and, uh, Ray, that was it. Raymond Smith, thick glasses with big black frames. Actually liked Calculus. I never did understand that kid."

Hunter stopped to gaze down into the water as it foamed over a kayak obstacle. "Although in Goshen, Yoder and Hochstetler were more common names than Smith, with the heavy Amish contingent, there definitely were some for-real Smiths." They started walking again.

"Oh, I'm not saying it's impossible or anything," Johanna said. "But even if I was able to locate the guy among the ten thousand other Smiths out there, what am I going to do? Call him up and insist he do the right thing by her?

Guy sounds like a jerk, doesn't he? She doesn't need him around. He'd probably be more hindrance than help. Who needs him? Besides, I don't want to talk about it anymore. It's too beautiful out here tonight. Let's just enjoy ourselves."

He couldn't fight that sentiment. It was definitely a night meant to be spent on seduction. A slight floral scent washed over them with the breeze. Hunter assumed it came from the spring blossoms somewhere nearby. Women liked that kind of stuff, didn't they? There were whole counters in the department stores devoted to perfumes and lotions, after all. Come to think of it, some of the light scent floating on the air might be Johanna herself.

Hunter turned his head and tried for an inconspicuous sniff. Yep. She smelled like flowers and spring. He nuzzled his face into her hair, brought his hand up from her shoulder to play with it.

"What are you doing?"

His hand dropped away and his head shot up. "Nothing. I was just...noticing your hair, actually."

Her hair? What was to notice about that? "It's just hair."

No it wasn't. It was silky and finely textured. It slipped through his fingers like gossamer threads. No point in sounding like a complete fool. Gossamer threads? Hunter cleared his throat. "Sorry. It feels nice, though. Smells good, too."

She'd probably insulted him. Charlie was right. She really didn't know how to act around a man. "It's all right. I guess I'm not used to being touched. Took me by surprise is all. You can feel it if you want."

Feeling like an idiot, Hunter let his hand immediately dive back into the silky tresses. "I guess I'm more of a toucher than I knew." As he ran his fingers through her hair, he was reluctant to make the drive back home. Here there was blessed anonymity. They were one of many romantically inclined couples out lost in the night, murmuring words covered by the sound of cascading water. They might as well be alone, so little attention was being paid by the other self-absorbed couples. Back home waited nothing but interruption and intent observation by the younger set, who'd like nothing better than to catch somebody— especially should the somebodies involved turn out to be the local parental authority figures—at such inappropriate behavior as a bit of smooching. Tough to perform under such conditions.

They passed under a viaduct. Several couples had stalled out there, arms wrapped around each other's necks, lips sealed together. Hunter found it too reminiscent of going "parking" with his buddies and all their respective dates. At their now-advanced ages, Hunter considered himself and Johanna too old to be necking out in public like that. Hunter kept going. Farther down the walkway he sighted a park bench. On the other hand...he guided Johanna over to it, slinging his arm along its back and, conveniently, around Johanna as well.

Johanna leaned into him, enjoying the close contact.

They sat silently for a while, drinking in the evening, the quiet and the host of stars.

"Just being able to sit still for more than ten seconds is really nice," Johanna finally said. So was snuggling against Hunter the way she was, although Johanna wasn't about to admit as much out loud. Too forward, she thought.

"You probably don't get much of a chance to just sit with everything you've got going, do you?" Hunter asked idly, twirling a lock of her hair around a finger.

"Not really," she admitted, taking a deep breath of the balmy night air. "But then, you'd know what that's like."

"I'm rapidly finding out. This is nice," he offered. He ran the back of two fingers lightly across her cheek. "Soft."

Johanna imitated his motion on Hunter. Lightly, she laughed. "Not so soft."

Hunter felt his chin. He'd shaved earlier, for all the good it had done. "No," he admitted ruefully. If he ever decided to grow a beard, there'd be no problem, that was for sure. Then, in a teasing motion, he rubbed his lightly stubbled cheek along the elegant line of her jaw. Instead of the laugh he expected—they were out in public, after all—Johanna caught her breath and bit back a moan.

Hunter cocked a brow. Well, well, this was interesting. Instead of being ticklish, Johanna appeared to enjoy a bit of whisker burn. He also had the revelation that while her skin should have been pickled from all the chlorine she soaked in daily, it wasn't. Instead of dry, Johanna's skin was smooth and delicate-feeling, like Hunter imagined a baby's would feel. Careful to not actually abrade her skin, he did it again with much the same result. Next he tried the soft tissue beneath her chin and the tender skin of her neck. The woman really moaned then and Hunter forgot all about any possible audience.

"Johanna," he muttered, catching her face between his two hands and kissing her. Only this time he wasn't accepting any chaste, closemouthed response. No, sir, Hunter teased the sealed line of her lips with his tongue, then slipped it through to play with Johanna's when she parted her lips slightly. "That's it," he murmured. "Oh, baby, that's it."

Hunter's heart was racing as it tried to keep up with his system's demand to pump harder and faster. If his system came with gauges the way an engine did, Hunter figured he'd be redlining about now. "From a couple of kisses?" he asked himself as blood pounded through his temples on its way to burning out his brain. Oh, man, he was in a bad way. This whole operation had begun as a campaign to get his poor orphaned niece and nephews a mother, surely the most altruistic of motives. He'd been willing to sacrifice himself on the altar of matrimony in a truly noble and self-less manner to secure this end.

But something had happened along the way.

Boy, had it ever.

Altruism had gotten lost somewhere down the line. If Hunter ever succeeded in clearing up the tangles of both Johanna's and his own life enough to actually get a ring on her finger, he would still be needing a nanny for the children.

The children would, in fact, be lucky if they ever saw Johanna, for he intended to keep her locked up in his bedroom for the first year at least. After the first twelve months, he'd sit down and reevaluate the situation, but frankly, he didn't hold a whole lot of hope for the second year, either. Nor the third, really.

Maybe by the time Mikie hit high school he might let Johanna out of the bedroom. Of course by then they'd be lucky if either one of them could walk, let alone have the children recognize them.

Hunter moved one hand down in search of Johanna's breast. His thumb grazed her nipple and Johanna inhaled sharply. Damn, but she was responsive. He wanted her. Badly. But a public park bench was not the place. Neither was home the place, not unless he wanted four little moppets in the bed with them. So where was the place?

Frustrated, he ran a hand through his hair, making it stick up in several different directions. He was not going to cheapen what he thought they could have together by renting a room in a hotel for half an hour, and they sure couldn't stay overnight. In fact, they really shouldn't leave Grace much longer with the munchkins. Maybe they'd all gone peaceably to bed for her and were even now sleeping like little angels, but Hunter had stopped believing in fairy tales and Santa Claus a long time ago. With a deep, heartfelt sigh, Hunter sat up.

"Johanna, in case you can't guess, I want you pretty badly."

Johanna shivered as the night air hit the skin Hunter had

warmed with his body. "I'm sorry," she said. "I didn't mean to lead you on like that. I—"

Teeth gritted, Hunter interrupted. "You didn't lead me on. I initiated it and I like to think I was doing a creditable job of convincing you to let me see things through, but it's the wrong time and the wrong place."

"Oh, but I—"

"I just want you to know that my intentions are honorable. I'm not Jim Slick—"

"Smith—"

"Whatever. The point I'm trying to make here is that had things proceeded to their logical conclusions just now, it was not the end I had in sight, all right? It would have been a stepping-stone along the way." Hunter looked at Johanna's face, taking in the look of total puzzlement she wore. "Do you have any idea what I'm talking about?"

Johanna nodded her head vigorously. "Sure, abso—no, not really."

Hunter sighed, got up from the bench and guided Johanna back to the car in silence. After bundling her inside, he rounded the front of the vehicle and slipped behind the wheel. Sticking the key into the ignition, he started the engine, then turned it back off once more. He turned to Johanna.

"I think we could be good together, Johanna, that's all I was trying to say. And not just in bed, either, although God knows we'd probably burn up the sheets there, which is a good thing. A very good thing. It just can't be the only thing a couple has going for them in a relationship."

Johanna's eyes widened. "Good together? You mean like you and me? Together?"

Hunter sighed again, this time with impatience. Why had the woman thought he'd been hanging around? he wondered. "Yes."

"Oh. Well. Uh—"

Hunter nodded to himself and restarted the car. *Yes. Oh, well and uh.*

Silence reigned in the car for a good fifteen minutes. They were almost back at his house before Johanna spoke. "I want you to know something, Hunter."

Hunter flicked on his turn signal and checked his mirrors before changing lanes. "What's that?"

"I wish the timing was better in my life because what you said before, you know, about us being good together, well that means something to me, you know? I mean, when you used the term *relationship,* that meant something permanent, right?" Johanna swallowed hard after biting the bullet. Guys did not like the p-word used in close proximity to the r-word. Johanna had noticed it tended to make them break out in a sweat. She also needed to be absolutely sure there was no miscommunication going on here, because the men who hadn't broken out in a sweat had been after something totally different from her.

"Most of the guys I come in contact with are swim parents. If they've got kids and are interested in dating, it's because they're divorced or the poor guy's wife died. I always got the feeling they were looking more for a combination baby-sitter, maid, chauffeur or a little one-on-one coaching for their potential Olympian, more than a partner. You feel for these fathers, but it still kind of stings that they're seeing you as a service provider instead of a person. Like I said, it stung some, but not a whole lot because I didn't see *them* that way, either. But with you, well I would have cared if you'd mentioned services you'd be gaining, instead of me, you know, as a person."

Johanna gestured vaguely with a hand, too embarrassed to say anything about how important she found it that she also turned him on. Now, that was exciting, a first in her life. "I just wanted you to know I really appreciate that. And like I said, I wish the timing were better, but with my mom and everything..." Her voice trailed off.

So, did he feel lower than a snake's belly or what?

"Yeah, I meant permanent. I sure as hell did. And those other guys were obviously a bunch of unthinking clods," he declared, and hoped like hell the warmth he felt wasn't his face flushing, and if it was, that the flush would go unnoticed in the dark car.

"That's what Mom said," Johanna laughed. "But she's supposed to think the opposite sex is blind and unappreciative when it comes to her children. As I've reached the ripe old age of twenty-five and am still unattached, she's convinced the male half of the population must be quite stupid." Johanna cast an uneasy glance his way as she listened to what she'd just said. "I mean, I'm sure your mother feels the same way. Um, right?"

Time to turn over a new leaf. Be a little more honest. Hunter took a deep breath. "My parents are both dead. Dad had a heart attack behind the wheel of a car. Drove right into a tree. He was already gone, they suspect, but the crash took Mom."

"I'm so sorry."

"Yeah, well, I wasn't exactly a baby at the time. I was twenty, in my sophomore year at college. I was a young, rebellious kid, really. Going out, having fun, getting in trouble." Hunter sighed. He tapped blunt fingertips on the steering wheel. "You never had a chance to rebel and get it all out of your system by being wild and crazy. Well, at least your parents didn't die thinking they'd been total failures where you were concerned."

Johanna automatically protested. "Oh, I'm sure they didn't—"

"Yeah, they did. They were fairly disgusted with me at the time. Reamed me up one side and down the other. To top it all off, I was on academic probation at the time. I was, uh, enjoying my college experience to the utmost at the time my parents died. My parents would die all over again if they knew I had a master's in business now and

was doing as well as I am. My dad pretty much told me
he figured I'd end up a street cleaner if I continued on my
current path. Work my way up to leaf sweeper.''

Hunter gave another heartfelt sigh as he thought back.
He hoped like hell his dad could see what he'd made of
himself, and that all the heavy-duty tuition his parents had
forked over hadn't been wasted after all. ''Anyway, thank
God for Robert and Mary Ellen. They were high school
sweethearts and never looked at another potential spouse
once they'd hooked up. Got married halfway through college. Didn't even slow them down. They both graduated
on time, both on the dean's list. Karen had just been born
when my parents went. She and Robby were the apples of
my parents' eyes. Along with Robert and Mary Ellen, of
course.''

''That must have been hard for you.''

''That Robert and Mary Ellen were constantly being held
up as the ideal I should be emulating? Nah, they were such
a great couple you couldn't hate them, and believe me I
wanted to. I tried. I was the original rebel without a cause
back then.'' Hunter pulled into his driveway, clicked the
garage door opener and slid his car inside. ''Let's just say
I hope I've matured some.''

''You know, you always think you've got the worst deal
in town until somebody else opens up. Not only does everybody else have a story to tell, but it's usually worse than
your own. Look at me, feeling all sorry for myself because
I never had the chance to go away to college and now
because my mom's expecting again. At least we're all
healthy and alive.''

''There's something to be said for that,'' Hunter agreed,
thinking about his parents and brother. He'd do just about
anything to have them back. Unfortunately, there wasn't
anything he could do and he was damn tired of struggling
with the impotency he felt when it came to railing against
the fates. Here it was again. The perfect woman, and no

matter how hard he fought, there was no way he was going to get her. Her sense of responsibility, which had been a key part of his initial reason for being drawn to her, was now going to keep them apart. Of all the rotten luck.

"Johanna, you're a damn attractive woman. I noticed that right off, I swear." Hunter switched off the engine and shifted uncomfortably. "But I've got to tell you, I also noticed how good you are with kids and I needed help with this crew. My motives weren't totally pure, I'm not going to lie."

Johanna was stunned. "But that doesn't make sense. I mean, when their parents come back..."

"Their parents aren't coming back."

Johanna swallowed. "Excuse me?"

"My brother and his wife were wonderful people, caring parents who'd never have left their children in a confirmed old bachelor's care for any length of time if they'd had a choice, Johanna. They're dead. I thought you knew that."

Johanna stared at Hunter. She clasped her two hands tightly together to keep them from trembling. "Dead?"

"Killed in a car crash. About the only good thing about the whole mess was that they didn't suffer. A triple trailer lost control, flipped on top of them. It was instantaneous."

Johanna was horrified. "It sounds awful, though I'm glad they didn't suffer."

Hunter ran a hand through his hair. "It *has* been awful— for the kids. They've been missing their parents, having nightmares, acting out." Hunter closed his eyes. "It's all I can do to keep my head above water. And damn it, I miss my brother."

Johanna turned to Hunter. She couldn't believe what she'd just heard. Her natural sympathy rose. "I'm so sorry."

Hunter pinched the bridge of his nose. "Yeah. Well. Thanks. Anyway, Johanna, what I mean is, well, those other guys? The swim fathers? They weren't just seeing a mother for their kids when they looked at you. No way. You're good with kids, true enough. But those guys probably thought they'd died and gone to heaven—just like I did—because you're also incredibly sexy, beautiful and fun to be with. Of course they want you. They're not stupid. Neither am I. But I understand your reservations. Really. I'd get the deal of the century by being with you whereas you…''

He sighed. Well, if he couldn't have her for keeps, he at least had her this evening. Turning to Johanna, he unfastened her seat belt. Then he pulled her close with every intention of kissing her blind. Johanna might as well know what she was missing. That way they could both toss and turn all night. It was fairer that way, he decided as his mouth descended. And he was nothing if not a fair man.

Pausing in his descent, he pushed his hand through her soft hair. ''Damn, you're beautiful.''

Suddenly the door between the garage and the house opened, interrupting them. The overhead light flicked on and Grace peered out the open doorway.

''Oh, good, I'm glad you're back. Hunter, I finally got Aaron and Mikie to bed. They're both passed out cold. But I'm having a little trouble with Karen and Robby. Robby won't stay in his own bed. He keeps running into Karen's room and farting. Then she says she can't stay in there because he's gassed the room out. As soon as I think I've got them settled down, it starts all over again. I don't know what to do. They're going to wake up Mikie and Aaron. How can Robby keep farting like that?''

''It's a gift,'' Hunter muttered. ''Most little boys his age have it. Especially if they have a sister they can harass by doing it.''

''Wouldn't you think he'd run out of gas sooner or later?''

''You'd think, but I wouldn't count on it.''

Johanna stared at him.

Hunter cleared his throat. "Ah, what you have to understand is that to the eight-year-old male mentality, burping and farting are about the funniest things to come down the pike, no lie."

"Yes, but—"

"I'm not kidding here, Johanna. Robby's probably going to have sore ribs tomorrow from doubling over in laughter. You've got to figure he's had Grace and Karen both going for quite a while now. Quite a coup when you stop and think about it." Hunter frowned as he thought about it. No longer being eight himself, the activity had lost a great deal of its humor.

Giving up on seduction in the garage, Hunter pulled the keys out of the ignition and opened his door then slammed it behind him. Retrieving Johanna from the passenger side, he directed her with a gesture of his hand to precede him into the house.

"All right, Grace, I'll take care of it," Hunter said. "Johanna, give me a few minutes to open some windows upstairs and lay down the law to my nephew. I'll be down shortly to say good-night and give Grace a little extra for combat pay. Don't go anywhere," he directed grimly as he took the steps to the second floor two at a time. "It won't take me long to ground Robby for the rest of his natural life."

A short while later as he escorted Johanna and Grace out to Johanna's car, Hunter declared, "Robby's behavior is actually a good sign," he lectured. It was just unclear whether he was trying to convince himself or Johanna. "It means they're getting comfortable with me, settling in. Robby no longer feels like he has to use his Sunday manners or run the risk of being turned out on his ear."

"Well, of course you wouldn't turn him out on his ear."

"He's too young to understand why his world has changed so. I've explained it over and over but I think he

still feels Robert and Mary Ellen deserted them, that if he'd
been better, they wouldn't have left.''

"Maybe it is a good sign, then," Johanna murmured, not
at all convinced that passing gas on command could—or
should—be used as an index of a child's good psychological adjustment. Perhaps she'd try to look it up in her old
child psych textbook. She'd found stranger things there. Or,
if she ever decided to go on for a master's, it might make
an interesting thesis for a paper, Johanna supposed. Original, at any rate. God, she felt awful. As if she'd been run
through an emotional wringer. "I'm sure Robby—and the
rest of them—will be okay again...some day.''

She stopped by the side of her car. "Well, good-night,
then," Johanna said, unsure of what else to say in light of
the evening's events. Thank you for asking me to marry
you? Except he hadn't, not in so many words, but what else
did permanent relationship imply? Now that she thought
about it, it could cover a lot of ground, so Johanna simply
shut her mouth and stopped with the good-night.

Hunter jammed his hands into his pants' pockets in a
gesture of sheer frustration. "Yeah, good n—oh, hell with
it." His hands streaked out of his pockets and he grabbed
Johanna and pulled her close. "Grace, don't let me hear
you repeating that and turn your head. I'm about to kiss
your sister silly and you're too young to watch.''

"I'm not—''

"Don't mess with me, Grace. I'm not in the mood. I'm
a desperate man.''

"Men are so strange," Grace huffed, and, crossing her
arms over her chest, turned her back on them. "Hurry it
up and get it over with, will you? I've had a rough night.
I want to go home.''

"I'll pay you for the overtime," Hunter growled, and
sealed his mouth over Johanna's.

When he was done, he had to steady Johanna as her legs
had gone limp as noodles. That at least pleased him. Prop-

ping Johanna up against her car, he pulled his wallet out of his back pocket. "You can turn around now," he told Grace, and handed her five more bucks. "That ought to cover it."

Johanna blew her bangs out of her face with a puff of air. "Don't you dare take that, Grace. Don't you dare."

Hunter curled Grace's hand around the bills. "Don't get into a twist over it, Johanna. It was worth it. Now, good-night, ladies. Be safe. Lock your doors, keep the windows up and drive straight home. Call me when you get there so I know you arrived all right." Sounding more like a parent every day, Hunter shook his head in disgust and stalked back to the house. He swiveled on the front porch to make sure the car started for Johanna. The coughing fit her motor produced when Johanna started her engine did not reassure him. He shook his head as her car drove off down the street.

Johanna drove home, her mind in a daze. She didn't follow boxing. Couldn't quite figure out who did or why they did. She had a vague recollection of her brothers going nuts years before when one boxer had bitten off another's ear in the ring. What kind of sport was that? No, Johanna had no idea who the current champion of the ring was, but she darn well knew how they felt. She, herself, felt as though she'd absorbed one body blow after another these past few days and was darn lucky to be able to stand, let alone function in a coherent fashion. Darn lucky.

Johanna put the car away. She and Grace wound their way through the darkened first floor of the house. A bass rhythm thumped down through the ceiling. Charlie was home. Sure. The one night she probably wouldn't be able to fall asleep to save her soul turns out to be the one night she doesn't have to sit up and wait to make sure no one missed their curfew. It just figured.

Saying good-night to Grace in the upstairs hall, Johanna sneaked into her own room. On the other side of the bookcase partition, a light shone. Johanna peeked around the corner.

"Mom? What are you doing awake so late?"

"It's only eleven-thirty, honey. I'm reading while I waited for you."

"Mom, you don't have to wait up for me. I'm twenty-five and you need your sleep."

Maddie shut her book. "I took a nap and intend to sleep in tomorrow morning. I also know I don't have to wait up for you. I wanted to. We haven't had a chance to talk alone in a long time."

Johanna felt a flash of guilt. Hadn't her mother told her she was lonely? Why hadn't Johanna made more time for her?

Maddie sat up and hugged her knees.

"Don't do that. You'll squash the baby or something. Won't you?"

Maddie gave her daughter a disbelieving look. "Maybe you're the one who needs a talk, Jo. The baby's maybe half an inch long. My sitting up isn't going to squash him or her. I did it with the rest of you, and you're all fine."

"Maybe me," Johanna grumbled. "I might be fine, but the rest of them are all nuts. I think you smushed their brains doing stuff like that when you were pregnant with them."

Maddie rolled her eyes. "How are your classes going? Any progress on the job queries or the apartment hunt? And most important, how was your date?"

Johanna sighed and sank down on the end of her mother's bed. "My classes are going well. Just think, after next week I'll never have to cram for another exam or turn out another term paper as long as I live."

Her mother laughed. "Don't get too excited. You'll be writing plenty of reports and things instead. You'll be longing for the days when all you had to do was stay up late for a single paper."

"Don't burst my bubble, Mom. Anyway, my date was incredibly confusing but wonderful and I have no intention of looking for an apartment. I'm not turning this household over to Charlie's care, not while you're in your condition. I'm staying here to be with you and the baby."

"Oh, no you're not."

"Oh, yes I am."

Maddie gave Johanna a baleful glare. "I should have guessed you were thinking along those lines. We'll get that straightened out later. In fact, tomorrow we'll go apartment hunting together. For now, tell me about the date. That Hunter is one good-looking man, isn't he?"

"Yeah, he is," Johanna agreed. How could she not? And because Johanna really didn't feel like arguing and really did need someone to talk to, she proceeded to dump the contents of her heart all over her mother's bed.

Chapter Ten

Maddie listened intently for a good twenty minutes. When Johanna's recital finally wound down, all she could say was "Wow. You've really got yourself tied up into a knot over all this, haven't you? Do you feel any better now that it's all off your chest?"

"No, not really," Johanna admitted miserably. "It's just all so hopeless."

"Yes, when your heart doesn't pay any attention to the plans you've got laid out for your life, it can be pretty miserable."

"It sucks. Big time."

"Watch your mouth, honey. The walls have ears around this place."

Johanna rolled her eyes. "Mom—"

"And none of that. Now, let's see what we can do to sort this mess out."

"Good luck," Johanna muttered.

"I suspect we'll need that, too, but mostly it's going to take determination and hard focusing on your goals."

"It's all so impossible," Johanna moaned, reveling in her misery.

"Now, stop that kind of talk. It's nothing of the kind. Love doesn't always choose to be convenient. Ask anyone and they're bound to have a story. Ask me, for crying out loud. You think I haven't been where you are? You think I don't know what you're going through? Well let me tell you, when I met your father the timing sucked big time, too."

Johanna was properly horrified. "Mother, your language."

"You think your generation thought up foul language? You think I don't know how to swear? I can do a whole lot better than that, if I put half a mind to it. I've always tried to give a good example to you children, but I'm quite capable of cutting loose if I so choose."

Johanna was beginning to believe it. Holy cow. Her mother was showing so many new sides of herself to Johanna that Johanna's head was all but spinning.

"I had plans laid out for my life, too, when I bumped into your father. And they didn't include seven children or supporting said children all on my own. Oh, no, I was planning on law school. I was planning on opening up my own firm and specializing in women's legal issues." Maddie gave a feminine version of a snort. "You can see how far I got. All I can say is that when life throws you a curveball, you stick your mitt up in the air and do your damnedest to field it. The solutions are seldom ideal, but you limp along doing the best you can. I never made it to law school, but the years I had with your father amounted to a life route I hadn't even contemplated seriously but never regretted taking for a minute. The time I had with your dad was very special. We fought and loved with equal passion. Now he's gone. Should I regret those choices because the time was brief? I don't think so. Should I regret having had seven children now that I'm on my own? Each one of you carries a part of your father. Some physical resemblance, some way of moving. Grace's eyes, Will's throw when he pitches a ball. Even with the benefit of hindsight I wouldn't change a thing. Not when I see bits and pieces of your dad in you all every day of my life. And which of you would I want to do without? Even-tempered Aubrey? Charlie with his impatience to go out and experience what life has to offer? Chris, who thinks he could solve world hunger along with any of our other problems large or small if we'd just pay a little more attention to what he has to say?''

Johanna blinked at her mother's vehemence. It would appear her mother was a lot stronger than Johanna had ever suspected. The strength of her convictions flowed through every word she spoke. Holy Mary.

''I changed my plans when love hit me in the face and I'm not sorry, sweetie. Not one bit. Now all of that being said, let's get back to your problem. You have to decide, Jo, honey, what you want more, to be on your own in an apartment and join the dating scene or to have a life with Hunter Pace, with all the mess that would entail?''

Johanna struggled with the question. ''I just don't know, Mom. I want both. I like his kids. I really do. Why couldn't I have met him a year from now?''

Her mother was ruthless. ''You didn't. You met him this year. So quit railing against what can't be changed and answer the question.''

''The psych books says a person has to work through all their stages of psychological growth or they stunt their development, stall out right there at the unfinished level. I should probably really be on my own for a while before I settle down. I haven't dated all that much, after all. Who'd want to be stuck in emotional adolescence for the rest of their lives? But if I do that, chances are I might never meet anybody like Hunter again, don't you think? I mean this could be my one and only opportunity.''

Johanna flung herself prone on the bed and put the back

of one hand to her forehead. Now it was Maddie's turn to roll her eyes.

"On the other hand, if I go for Hunter now, I'm asking for trouble later because I'm skipping a stage, psychologically speaking. Probably have a hell of a midlife crisis or something. Maybe even have an affair," Johanna predicted darkly. "Multiple affairs." Johanna shivered in delicious horror as she imagined the forbidden scene. "Gross." She pointed a finger at her mother. "And that wouldn't be fair to Hunter when you stop and think about it. He's such a great guy. So giving, so loving. Look at the way he's caring for his brother's kids. If I hurt him, well, I'd just never forgive myself."

Maddie's mouth hung open. "That is the most incredible amount of drivel I've ever heard. You've read entirely too many psych books, that's your problem. You even think about having an affair regardless of whether you're fifty or thirty and I'll murder you. Think about the psychological scars *that* would leave on those children. No, you'll just have to stay repressed, that's all. Deal with your problems and skipped stages the best you can just like the rest of the world does."

"Easy for you to say. I may not be able to help myself."

"I wish I had a tape recorder to play this conversation back for you. You should just hear how ridiculous you sound."

Johanna had to allow for that possibility. "Maybe. If it was just the two of us, that would be one thing, but I really, really want to get away from anybody under the age of twenty-one right now."

"I can't blame you there," Maddie said. "Many is the time I've felt the same."

Grace came through the bedroom door, naturally without knocking.

"Grace, what are you doing in here?" Johanna snapped. "Mom and I are trying to talk."

Grace was unfazed. "Oh, I decided to stay up and finish some homework so I don't have to do it tomorrow, only I left my copy of the periodic table in my locker. Do either of you guys know the electronic charge on chlorine in its ionic state?"

"Minus one. I think."

"Calcium?" asked Grace as she scribbled quickly in the notebook she carried.

"Minus two. No, wait. It could be plus two. Oh, I don't know. Just go to bed."

"Johanna," her mother said. "Get a grip. Grace, how did your baby-sitting job go tonight?"

Grace rolled her eyes. "It was evil. Mikie started crying tonight when he saw you and Hunter drive off. Said he wanted his mommy and daddy. Aaron told him he couldn't have them, not ever again. That they were both in heaven with God and his angels. Mikie wanted to know how to get there. Said he wanted to see them real bad and Robby jumped in, laying it on real thick. Lots of nevers and ever agains. Then Mikie and Aaron both started crying. *I* started getting teary-eyed because I started thinking about our dad. Man, it really sucked with everybody wailing like that."

"Grace, don't say sucked," Johanna automatically corrected her. Then the sheer hopelessness of the situation sank in. "Ahh!"

"See?" Grace said. "I told you it sucked."

"You heard your sister, Grace. Don't say sucked."

Johanna slept poorly that night. In fact, when the sun rose the following morning she wasn't sure she'd slept at all. She was pathetically grateful when the gray light of early morning filtered into the room. Rising, Johanna pulled a corner of the shade up and peeked out the window. The sun hung over the horizon, no more than a glow behind a bank of clouds and looking much like a reluctant riser itself. "Yeah, good morning to you, too," Johanna muttered, and let the shade drop back into place. She toed her slippers on and went downstairs to start some coffee. As she sipped, Johanna began to compose her list for the day's chores.

"Let's see. I need to figure out the relays for next weekend's meet. I'll have to allow time to get over to Hunter's sometime and murder him for making me care so much about him, kids and all. I've got the rough draft on the paper for abnormal psych to finish. Murder's really too good for him. It's so over and done with. Torture might be a better choice. Charlie and Chris are going to have to help me make plans for finishing up a corner of the basement since they'll be living down there. If I'm staying, I get a room to myself. The baby can share with Mom when it gets here. But what kind of torture? Something really painful, I'm thinking. Hmm…"

That was how her mother found her. "Johanna?"

"Hmm?"

"What are you doing up so early? It's six in the morning."

"Hmm? Oh, just thinking. Planning. You know?"

Maddie glanced down at the open newspaper and cold coffee in front of her daughter. The paper was open to a hardware ad. "That's the wrong section," she pointed out, and reached in front of Johanna to ruffle through the paper. "Here. Apartments for rent will be in this part. Somewhere," Maddie said as she flipped pages.

"Mom, what would you think about finishing off a part of the basement for Charlie and Chris? Their room makes the whole upstairs hallway smell like dirty socks, and how much can a couple of sheets of drywall cost?" Johanna asked as she tapped the hardware store advertisement.

"It's not a bad idea, I guess, although I made them clean out under their beds, and it doesn't smell nearly as bad in their room now. They pulled out some dirty underwear and a few stray socks that must have slipped under there when they weren't looking," Maddie answered absently as she searched a kitchen drawer for a pen and poured herself a glass of milk.

"Since when do you drink milk?" Johanna asked as her mother sat down beside her and began perusing the paper.

"Since I can't remember if coffee's all right for unborn babies. All that caffeine, you know. Don't want the poor kid born a jittering idiot. I know milk's okay so I'll stick with that till I get to the doctor's. Now, here's one, Jo. Garden apartment, one bedroom. I think this address is down by the river. Could be a nice view."

Johanna sat back and stared. Her mother, the unwed mother. Holy cow. Then she keyed in to what her mother was saying.

"This one might be worth checking out, too," Maddie said as she circled a second ad.

"Mom, I'm staying here, remember? That's why we're going to finish up a corner of the basement—so Charlie and Chris can move downstairs and I can have their room."

"We're finishing off the basement so Charlie and Chris can move downstairs. I'm with you that far. Theirs is the biggest bedroom after the one you and I share. Once their room is open, we'll paint it something a little more feminine and Aubrey and Grace can move in. Their room is the smallest as well as the one closest to mine. That'll be the nursery. With you off on your own, it's going to be weird having a room all to myself again."

"Mom—"

Maddie gave her a sharp look. "No, Jo, you are not changing your plans. I've decided to try and contact Jim. He deserves to at least be informed of his impending fatherhood. What he does with that information is his choice. Doesn't matter. You're still moving out. You have six siblings, all quite capable of stepping up and filling in the gap. You just have to let them. You can't do for them forever, honey."

"They're all still in school full-time. What are you going to do with the baby while you're at work?"

"I'll hire a sitter for school-time hours. I'm in a different position than I was all those years ago when your dad died. I'm making better money and can get child care."

Johanna stared at her mother. It was disconcerting to be so easily dismissed. Since her father had died seven long years ago, Johanna had felt pretty much like Cinderella and had spent a lot of time feeling sorry for herself in her role as Cinderella, queen drudge. But what could she do? Her family had needed her. Now her mother was insisting on giving her just what she wanted. Her freedom. She'd also absolved Johanna of any guilt or responsibility for taking it. What could be better?

So, did Johanna feel ecstatic?

Was she jumping with joy?

Running out to buy paint for the apartment she'd decorated a hundred times over in her dreams?

None of the above.

Now she felt unappreciated. Go figure. Didn't her mother realize Johanna was indispensable? That without her the family couldn't possibly function correctly? Well, fine. If that's the way they were going to be, let them try and get along without her, the ungrateful slobs. They'd be calling her home within a week, see if they didn't.

Johanna took the apartment-for-rent ads and went to get dressed.

All week long, Johanna nervously looked for Hunter at the practices. She both wanted and didn't want to see him at the same time. The man never showed his face. "Go figure," Johanna muttered.

"So, where's your uncle?" she subtly questioned Karen as the little swimmer handed Johanna her goggles with a request for adjustment. Friday had rolled around and there was still no sign of the man.

"We joined a carpool," Karen informed her with a disdainful sniff as water dripped down her legs, making her huddle in on herself and shiver. "We got to ride home with Billy and his mom."

Johanna wouldn't want to ride home with Billy, either. Billy was all boy. In other words, the kid was totally hyperactive. "Oh. I see. I was just wondering, since he always used to come in and stay."

Robby, who'd come over to watch the operation on Karen's goggles, piped in, "Uncle Hunter says now that he's seen you in action he trusts you with us. He said there wouldn't be a swimming pool left if he kept bringing Aaron and Mikie."

"That's 'cuz Aaron and Mikie are always wreckin' stuff," Karen informed Johanna.

"Uh-huh." Johanna shrugged nonchalantly. "Like I said, I was just wondering."

She was starting to feel neurotic. On one level she wanted him to pursue her. On another, she wanted him as far away as possible. He'd come after her to find a mother for his kids, after all. He'd come right out and admitted as much. She watched as the siblings jumped back in the pool. Well, the man had a legitimate excuse. Mikie and Aaron probably would destroy the pool complex given enough time. They certainly had the energy for the task.

"I'll confront him tomorrow," she told herself after she got her group going on a set of twenty-five-yard sprints. Sprints was a misnomer for the eight and unders, as even one length of the pool all out took a while for a little kid. "He's not going to give up a Saturday of free baby-sitting. He'll show up."

Johanna went home that evening to pack a few more boxes of her things. She'd been lucky enough to find a sublease on an apartment. It was furnished, so she wouldn't have to scrounge around for furniture or anything. Sure she'd have to move the end of August when the real renters came back, but by then her family would have come to its senses and realize how much they needed her. "And if they're still all stubborn and hardheaded, I'll find another place. But this way we've got almost four months to try things out and see how it goes. Better than being tied into some long-term lease," she reassured herself as she fell into bed.

Bright and early the next morning, Johanna bounced up and jumped into the shower. She could hardly wait for Hunter to show up. "What is wrong with you, girl," she asked the face in the mirror, her words coming out slightly garbled due to the toothbrush in her mouth. "The man only wanted help with his brood—a mommy essentially—and you're getting all dolled up." She shook her head as she realized how easy it had been to swallow Hunter's assurance that he'd been primarily attracted to her and the mothering would have been a side benefit. "Hah!"

Someone pounded on the bathroom door.

"Hey, Jo?"

It was Chris. "Hey, what?"

"That Hunter dude called while you were using up all the hot water."

Johanna spit and rinsed. "Yeah? What'd he want?"

"Said to tell you one of the motley monsters, I forget which one, is running a temp and has severe crabitis. They're not coming. Said he'd take a rain check."

"That's what he thinks," Johanna muttered to her reflection, determined to face him. "I don't give rain checks. It's now or never. After tomorrow, I'll be out of here and nobody under an age that can be legally held responsible for any damage they do to my new place will be allowed in."

"What?"

"Okay, I heard you. Thanks for the message."

"Maybe you should call him back if and when you ever get out of there. Fevers in young children can be serious, you know. Fry their brains. They can go into convulsions and die.''

''Thank you, Dr. Durbin.''

''Probably ought to make sure he knows about aspirin and Reye's syndrome, too.''

''All *right,* Christopher.''

Johanna could almost hear her brother's shrug. ''Just trying to help.''

''Thank you. Now I'm going to dry my hair. Go away.''

But Johanna didn't call Hunter. He was a grown man quite capable of handling a little bug in the house. How hard was chicken soup and aspirin substitute, after all? But she felt really guilty when Monday practice came and only Karen showed up, dropped off by Billy's mother, much to her disgust. An educated guess had Robby being the one running the fever on Saturday.

''Robby still sick, Karen?'' she asked. Three days was a long time. Maybe she should have called.

Karen gave her a puzzled look. ''Robby's not sick.''

''He's not?''

''Nah. He had to go to school tonight for the third-grade play.''

''Oh. He's feeling better then.''

''Robby was never sick, Coach Jo. Maybe you're thinking of Aaron. Uncle Hunter made him sit in the bathtub most all today and yesterday.''

Good grief. How high a fever was the child running? Surely he should see a doctor if he still needed cooling three days later.

''The doctor told Uncle Hunter to make Aaron sit in the tub with that stuff in the water you use for making cookies.''

Now she was totally confused. ''What stuff is that, Karen?''

''You know. That white powdery stuff in the little yellow box. Uncle Hunter bought boxes and boxes of it. It makes the water all cloudy when he dumps it in. But know what? I don't get why putting that stuff in the water makes you less itchy. And when Aaron's not in the tub? Uncle Hunter puts this pink goo all over him. He sure looks funny, but Uncle Hunter says not to laugh 'cuz probably the rest of us are all gonna have spots just like that come next week.''

The light dawned. ''Aaron has chicken pox?''

''Does he ever. He's got spots on top of his spots, Uncle Hunter says. He says at the rate things are going he's never gonna get back to his office 'cuz we'll probably get our spots one at a time just to spite him and he may have to tell, tella, tell something with his computer forever.''

Poor Uncle Hunter. ''Telecommute?''

''Yeah, that.''

''I wonder why he didn't call?'' Johanna asked herself out loud after starting her squad off on a stroke drill. She had distinct memories of her mother being ready to pull out her hair by the time she'd nursed the younger ones through their bout with chicken pox. Talk about cranky! And trying to keep them from scratching was a nightmare. And once it started in a household, it would work its way through. With an eight-to-ten day incubation period, an infection that ran over a week itself and four children, why, Hunter could be housebound for close to two months.

Johanna knocked over a stack of kickboards and swore under her breath. ''I'd be an idiot to go over there.'' Her newfound split personality kicked in. But why hasn't he called? First my mom doesn't need me and now Hunter? I thought he needed a mother for those kids. What am I, chopped liver? I can mother. Isn't it just like a man to go all stubborn on you when you least expect it? I'll just stop over there on my way home. No I won't. Well, maybe I should just make sure they don't need anything from the store. I could...''

Johanna dropped the fins into their bin and did a visual sweep of the pool deck. She picked up two pairs of goggles and a ripped cap with a snarling shark on the side. "Oh, man, the next person who tells me I have a way with young children dies," she promised herself.

"I won't say it. I don't want to die."

Johanna whirled around. "Grace!" She hugged her sister even though she'd just seen her the day before. "How's it going?"

Grace screwed up her face into a grimace. "Terrible. You've only been gone one day and I really, really miss you."

Ah, see there? She'd known they couldn't get on without her.

"Charlie forgot to remind us to make our lunches last night so we were all scrambling like mad this morning. I almost missed the bus. And there aren't going to be any cookies for tomorrow's lunches because nobody picked it out off his new job chart thing he's starting."

Johanna's brow furled. "So why don't you trade in whatever job you've got and take care of it yourself?"

"I don't want to bake cookies. That job takes twice as long as vacuuming the floor. I told Charlie and Chris they should do it since they're older and we'd all starve to death at this rate, but Charlie says he's the slave driver now and he doesn't have to do stuff like that and we'll all adjust."

Johanna swallowed. "And what about Chris?"

"He said something about how things are always confusing at first when new management comes in with a different management style and technique and walked away."

Sounded like law and order in the Durbin household was going to hell in a handbasket. "Did you talk to Mom about this?"

"She just mumbled something about Charlie doing things differently didn't make it wrong, just different, and how she couldn't undermine his authority. She said if worse came to worst we'd buy cookies from the store. But I don't like store-bought cookies, Johanna. You know that. You've got to do something."

Johanna recognized that she couldn't undermine her brother's authority, either. He wasn't doing anything life-threatening. In that her mother was right. It just wasn't the way she would have handled things. So while Johanna wanted to run home and get things back on track, her term as president of the household was over and she'd been kicked out of the White House. It hurt her feelings that things weren't in a legitimate uproar without her. Everyone needed to be needed, but there you were. Grace was old enough to remember to make her own lunch and the health board would not issue a citation if they had to survive on store-bought cookies.

"I can't, honey," Johanna admitted with a sigh. "Not unless Mom asks. Let's just wait a little longer and see how things go, all right?"

But she went back to her silent, quiet apartment with a heavy heart. She sat on the living room sofa. This was what she'd wanted. This was what she'd prayed for during all the craziness of running her childhood home.

A little peace and quiet.

"Only now I've got a *lot* of peace and quiet and you know what? It's too damn quiet in here." Johanna was rapidly discovering that a little peace and quiet went a long way.

She turned on the TV, then went into the kitchen to make her supper. She was more comfortable working with the sound in the background even though she had no idea what show was on. She just needed the noise. Johanna cooked way too much food. "It's going to take a while to adjust to cooking for only one," she reassured herself. "After all, I'm used to cooking for eight."

Storing the leftovers, she was suddenly struck by an awful thought. "Does this mean I can never have apple pie again?" she asked herself as she stared into the almost-empty refrigerator. "If I bake a whole pie, I'll be fat as a pig in no time because I'll know it's there and I'll eat it all and you can't bake just one slice, now can you?"

You can buy pie by the slice at the store, stupid, she told herself. "But I don't like store-bought pie," Johanna heard herself whining, and knew it was time to put herself to bed with a book. Paradise, she was rapidly discovering, had a few thorns.

By the end of that week Johanna had to make a concentrated effort to go back to her apartment after practice. She wanted to go home and join in the bedlam sure to be found there. But she had to stay away and not undermine Charlie. Stephen had called to complain he'd gotten a D on a spelling test and it was all Charlie's fault for not making him study. Charlie had shrugged and told Stephen his grades were his personal responsibility. If he didn't like getting D's he knew what he could do about it, Charlie had proclaimed before walking away.

It made a certain amount of sense.

But if she went home, she'd stick her oar in. Johanna was more hands-on than Charlie, that was all, she thought.

The apartment was still too darn quiet. You could hear every creak and groan the building made.

Thursday, Karen stopped coming to practice. Robby made it through Friday but was among the missing the following Monday. Hunter was juggling at least three cases of chicken pox and still hadn't called to ask for help. What in the world was wrong with the man? Didn't he know when he was overwhelmed? Or was he one of those stubborn types who would rather pass out than cry uncle?

Johanna had two job interviews set up for Tuesday. She couldn't get Hunter and his predicament out of her head and was afraid she'd seemed flaky. During Wednesday's interview she was so distracted she actually had to have a school principal repeat his question. Twice.

"That does it," she muttered under her breath as she

strode out of the building. "He's got me so worried I can't concentrate. These people will never call me back, that's for sure. This is all Hunter's fault. Of all the inconsiderate—" Johanna ran out of adjectives evil enough to cover one Hunter Pace about the same time she noticed a class of kindergartners coming in from recess staring at her.

Johanna rolled her eyes. "Great, even the five-year-olds think I'm mental. Wonderful." She climbed into her car and started the engine. "Well, let's just see about that. Thinks he can take me out to dinner one night and ignore me the next three weeks? He's got another think coming, let me tell you." And she drove directly to Hunter's home, anxious to have it out with him face-to-face. "Either he wants me or he doesn't. Either he needs me to help him with the kids or he doesn't. What's it going to be?"

Johanna rang the bell and, when it didn't instantly open, pounded on the door.

"For crying out loud, who—" Hunter wrenched the door open and scowled at Johanna. "Johanna! What's the matter?" He stepped out onto his stoop and glanced in both directions. "Somebody hassling you out here? Why are you banging like that?"

Johanna poked her index finger into Hunter's chest and had him retreating back into the house. "Why didn't you call me when the kids got sick? What, after a couple of months you're already in the running for the Father Knows Best Award? Well, you look like hell. What is it with you men? Why can't you ever admit you need help?" Johanna's tirade was interrupted by a loud crash over their heads. "What was that?"

Hunter caught her hand in one of his to stop the poking. "I don't know. I don't want to know. God, I hope it wasn't one of their heads." He went to the bottom of the stairs and called up. "Karen?"

"Yeah?"

"What was that noise?"

"Nothing."

Hunter ran a hand through his hair in a distracted gesture. "I hate it when they say that."

"Hunter, you're about to fall over right where you stand. Why didn't you call?"

"Johanna, I have three children upstairs in full-bloom chicken pox and Mikie is irritable as hell, which means he'll probably start breaking out by tomorrow. I wouldn't ask my worst enemy to help me out and you're hardly that. Don't worry about the kids. I'm in contact with a pediatrician and everything is running the way it should. For chicken pox. They'll be fine."

Johanna studied the blue circles under Hunter's eyes and the fine lines of fatigue around his mouth. "I'm not worried about the kids, I mean I'm concerned about them, certainly, but I'm much more worried about you. You look exhausted. How about if I—"

"No," Hunter said firmly. He took her shoulders and turned Johanna around so she was facing the front door. "I've done a lot of thinking since that night we went to South Bend, Johanna. I freely admit my initial attraction came from less-than-altruistic motives. You've got a body a man could die getting his fill of and a real knack for dealing with children. It was an irresistible combination. But as I've gotten to know you better, I've come to realize how selfish it would be for me to pursue a relationship. All these years you've done nothing but give. Here you are, so looking forward to being out on your own, to making up for all the time you think you've lost on the dating scene. You've never had a chance to do the first-apartment thing, the first-job thing. I want you to have all of that, which means I have to back off."

Hunter was walking her to the door as he spoke, his arm around her shoulder. "I want to snatch you up before any of those other jerks with their motherless kids get to you, but I want a whole bunch of things. A red Corvette, a ski lodge in upper Michigan." He opened the front door. "It's killing me to be this noble, Johanna. I must have an innately selfish streak in me I wasn't even aware of. You're going to have to help me here. Go home, okay?"

"Uncle Hunter?"

"Yeah, Robby?"

"I gotta go to the bathroom."

"Okay, champ, I'll be right there."

Johanna arched a brow. "Isn't he a little old to need help to the bathroom?"

"The bottoms of his feet are so broken out there isn't a clear spot to be found. He's got pox on top of pox on top of pox down there. It's really painful for him to walk so I carry him to the bathroom." Hunter shrugged. "It makes him feel better."

And Hunter would always strive to give that extra bit of caring, Johanna realized. Reaching out, she put her hand on his arm. "Hunter, you can't possibly cope. Let me—"

"No, if I get desperate, I'll hire somebody. My brother and sister-in-law's accident happened on the way home from a business dinner. It was work-related so Robert's insurance paid triple indemnity. The kids are set for life, I can afford whatever they need. College is all put away for them, although I'm sure they'd rather have their parents. Instead they're stuck with me." Hunter grimaced. "But we're getting used to one another."

"Uncle Hunter!"

"Coming, Robby," he called. "Go home, Johanna. They'll be all right and so will I. Enjoy yourself. You've earned every right to think of nothing but yourself now." And Hunter closed the door right in Johanna's face.

She stood there and stared at it briefly.

This was ridiculous.

Everything she'd wanted for so long was hers. Her own apartment with her own bedroom shared with nobody. No younger siblings running through her own private bedroom to borrow her stuff or ask her the electronic charge of calcium in its ionic state at odd hours of the day or night. She could eat pizza or guzzle pop for breakfast, lunch and dinner, if she so chose, without concern of giving a bad example. She was about to embark on an actual career, finally. And, if she decided to, she could stage week-long reenactments of Roman bacchanalian orgies if it struck her fancy.

So why was she standing in front of a closed door feeling abandoned, unloved and sorry for herself?

It was ridiculous.

She ought to go home and invite everyone she knew over for a giant party. A never-ending party. Maybe she'd finally get drunk herself. She was twenty-five. It was time. Johanna pivoted and marched down the front sidewalk and got into her car for the drive home.

Johanna had to turn the lights on when she walked into her apartment. That would never happen at home. Maybe she'd buy herself a timer so there'd at least be a welcoming light on when she returned. Was that asking so much? A welcoming light?

My, wasn't she having a pity party. But darn it, she didn't want to have a party. She'd never much cared for the Roman Empire's philosophy of life and wouldn't know how to throw a decent orgy to save her soul. Johanna wanted to be with Hunter, wiping fevered brows and spooning out chicken noodle soup.

Go figure.

She wandered around the house irritably kicking at defenseless inanimate objects, wishing someone would come over and do something, anything so she could tell them to stop. Johanna went to bed early, still out of sorts with the world and the beginnings of what promised to be a riproaring headache. She got up several times during the night, adding an extra blanket, then an hour later ripping everything but the sheet off, wet with sweat. By morning Johanna knew she was coming down with something or another.

"Oh, yeah," she muttered, squinting as the morning sunlight that leaked in around the edges of the bedroom's window shade all but blinded her. Her head started throbbing right where it had left off the night before. "Just what I need. A virus. Oh, joy."

No job interviews were on tap for the day, so instead of cleaning the already-clean apartment, Johanna stayed in bed feeling sick and sorry for herself.

By eight o'clock that night, Johanna had figured out it wasn't the twenty-four-hour kind of bug and was hoping for a forty-eight. She really couldn't afford much more time than that, not if she wanted to pay the rent much longer. At eight-thirty when the security buzzer rang, she ignored it. It was a school night and unlikely to be a family member. And Johanna didn't want anybody outside the family to see her like this, still in her pajamas, bed-head hair and generally rumpled-looking. Whoever it was had probably rung the wrong apartment, anyway.

Two minutes later, somebody banged on her door. It was Hunter's voice bellowing out her name. "Johanna! Open up!"

Johanna lurched up in surprise from the sofa where she'd been lying and then caught her head in her hands, moaning. The sudden move had set her headache off again.

"Johanna!"

"All right," she answered, pulling the sheet and blankets that were twisted around her legs free before she tripped. "I'm coming. Hang on. I'm coming. Just a sec."

Bleary-eyed, she opened the door, hanging on to its edge for support. "What d'you want?"

In a move that under different circumstances Johanna might have considered masterful and yes, even romantic, Hunter slid his hands up under her arms and simply picked her up. He carried her, feet dangling, back into her small living room, kicking the door shut with his foot. "What are you doing here, all alone, sick? Why haven't you called someone? Why the hell didn't you call *me* and let me know you were ill? What's wrong with you, anyway? You're burning up. Have you seen the doctor? You look terrible. What's his number?"

Johanna hung there in his arms gaping. The man had flipped out, gone around the bend. "Get a grip," she advised. "I've got the flu or something. I've lived through it before. I imagine I'll pull through this time as well."

"You shouldn't be by yourself."

Johanna shrugged. "Better than giving it to anybody else, although working with kids the way I do they're probably already exposed to whatever I've got. Heck, one of them no doubt *gave* it to me in the first place."

Hunter got an odd look on his face. "What did the doctor say when you called?"

Johanna rolled her eyes. "Hunter, I don't call the doctor every time I get a fever or a headache." She pointed to the glass on the end table. "I'm drinking fluids, taking a fever reducer and dozing off and on in front of old movies. I don't need to consult some high-priced medical degree to figure that out."

After finally lowering her to the floor, Hunter ticked her symptoms off on his fingers. "You have a headache, you're running a temperature and you're crabby as hell."

Johanna took immediate insult. "I am not the one in need of a personality adjustment here. You pushed your way in here with some kind of problem."

Hunter immediately dismissed any such notion. "You've had a bad attitude since I rang the bell."

"Pounded on the door is more like it," she sniffed. "I'm surprised it held and didn't cave right in."

Now he rolled his eyes and cut to the chase. "Whatever. Johanna, have you ever had the chicken pox?"

"Of course I have. You don't see any spots, do you?"

Then she had to slap at his hands when he reached for her pajama shirt and tried to lift it. "What are you doing? Stop it!"

"You break out first on the warm, covered areas of the body. I want to check your stomach and chest."

"In your dreams. Listen, if I want a second opinion, I'll pay a professional. Hunter, stop it, I mean it."

Totally ignoring her, Hunter picked Johanna up and laid her gently on the couch. Despite her good physical condition, Johanna was no match for him. She blamed it on her illness.

"Aha!" Hunter crowed, getting her shirt up despite Johanna's efforts to hinder him and pointing to something on her torso.

"What?" Johanna craned her neck, but couldn't really see anything. "Aha, what?"

"Aha, spots. Three of them. Look. Here, here and here."

"That's ridiculous. I don't have spots." But her hand was already moving to an itchy area on her midriff.

"Don't scratch them, you'll only make it worse." He began bundling her in the sheet and blanket from the couch. "Come on, I'm taking you home with me. I've got a year's supply of baking soda and soothing lotion put in. I'll take care of you. I know what to do." Without further ado, ignoring the hands batting at him and the loud protests ringing in his ear, Hunter carted her off.

Forty minutes later she was installed in Hunter's king-size bed with a pitcher of water, a mug of broth and a stack of magazines on the nightstand beside her. Hunter had taken her temperature, bundled her under blankets and called her mother. Her mother, for God's sake. And her mother had been no help whatsoever. None. She had informed Hunter that while Johanna had indeed had chicken pox as a youngster, it had been a very light case. Both her mother and the doctor had wondered at the time if it had been enough to induce immunity.

They all thought they had the answer to that question now, Johanna thought with a sniff. Hunter was off running her a bathtub full of water to soak in. With the information gleaned from her mother, Hunter had ruled out all other possibilities. He'd decided she was coming down with chicken pox and was running very much in man-on-a-mission mode.

"You'd think I was dying," Johanna muttered as Mikie, now in full-bloom pox, climbed under the sheets with her while Robby, Karen and Aaron sat on the bottom of the bed.

"How'd your uncle even find out I was sick, you guys?" she asked, still unable to believe the way he'd whisked her off. And the sad part was, she'd let him! That alone told Johanna how ill she must be. Just because Hunter had discovered the switch to some latent caveman gene didn't mean she had to go along with things, now did it? This was the twenty-first century, after all.

Karen answered her query. "I was bored. Uncle Hunter said I could call Aubrey and see if Kyle Neuburger snuck his new puppy into school the way he said he was gonna. I wanted to know if he got expelled or anything."

"Uh-huh. So did he?"

"Nah, he chickened out. I knew he would, but I just wanted to be sure, you know? Anyway, Aubrey said how you'd missed practice and mean Coach Jess had done the eight and unders and how I should be glad I had the chicken pox and wasn't there 'cuz it was really, really hard."

"Uh-huh. You mentioned my missing practice to your uncle, I take it?"

"Yeah, and did he ever get mad!"

"Mad?"

"Yeah, he was yelling and everything. Uncle Hunter said you could teach stubborn to a mule and you could probably be dying or something and wouldn't pick up the phone to ask for help."

"I wasn't dying," Johanna muttered. Her, stubborn. Well she liked that. Anyone with eyes could see that Hunter was the stubborn one. Good grief. Johanna shrugged. So now she knew how Hunter had found out. The rest Johanna already knew. "So he called a neighbor in to watch all of you while he came racing over on his white horse to rescue me from myself, is that it?"

"No, Coach Jo, he took our new car," Aaron answered seriously. "And it's red because Uncle Hunter said you can see red from farther away than most other colors. He said that's why a lot of ambulances are red and he wanted us all to be safe 'cuz he loves us and would be sad if anything happened to any of us."

"Of course he does, honey. Your uncle's life would be very boring without you four."

"Yeah," Aaron agreed, with Robby and Karen chirping right in.

"That's what he said."

"And it's true."

"All right, I told all you guys to let Johanna rest, didn't I?" Hunter said, standing in the doorway. "What're you all doing in here?"

"We weren't doing nothing, Uncle Hunter, honest."

"Yeah, Coach Jo was bored. We were cheering her up."

Hunter rolled his eyes. "God help her." He came over to the bed and scooped Johanna up in a move that seemed to be becoming second nature to him. Johanna immediately steadied herself by flinging her arms around his neck. He grinned at her. "I've got you, not to worry."

That's exactly what *did* worry her.

"Everybody, scat. Johanna's going to soak in the tub for a while. No visitors allowed. Except me."

"How come you get to stay?" Karen demanded.

"I've got to make sure she doesn't drown."

Robby snorted. "Coach Jo isn't going to drown, Uncle Hunter. She's a swim coach."

"Yeah, but she's sick so I've got to lifeguard her. Do I ever leave you guys alone in the tub? Do I?"

"Well, no."

"See there? This is all just part of my job description. Robby, take everybody downstairs and put on a movie. I won't be long."

Hunter shut the bathroom door on four little faces. He sat on the closed lid of the toilet, Johanna still in his arms, and breathed deeply of her unique fragrance. "Damn, it scared me when I heard you'd missed practice. Aubrey told Karen you never miss, no matter what."

She must really be ill. Instead of going into a lecture on how she could take care of herself, Johanna snuggled in to Hunter's chest. "It was always such bedlam at home, I'd be too sick to stay there. I kept going with my daily routine out of self-defense."

Hunter chuckled quietly. Here in the quiet of the bathroom with Johanna on his lap, cranky though she was, he was finally able to relax. "I know what you mean. I'm discovering the same thing."

Johanna closed her eyes and sighed contentedly. She let her fingers drift up and down Hunter's neck. "My head's killing me," she said. "And I itch. Can we just stay like this forever? I don't think I ever want to move again." One eye popped open. "Hunter, what about you? Have you had chicken pox?"

Now that he had Johanna in his arms under his eagle eye, Hunter was feeling fairly mellow himself. "Yeah, a good solid case when I was ten." He rubbed his cheek on the top of her head.

"Hunter?"

"Hmm?"

"You've got your hands full here. You don't need me adding to your troubles."

"Yes," Hunter said. "I do."

That stopped her short. "You do? Why?"

Hunter squeezed her briefly. "I thought it would be enough for me to step back. Let you have what would make you happy, your freedom. Time to just be, to discover who and what you are. But when I heard you were sick, I freaked."

"So the kids were saying."

"Big mouths," he grumbled, and Johanna giggled, kissing him lightly.

"Don't be mad. And you have to have known Mom was checking up on me. Charlie stopped by on his way to school, Chris on the way home. No doubt Mom herself would have shown up if I'd still been sick tomorrow."

"You're going to be down and out for a good week, sweetheart. Don't look now, but your neck is breaking out. And you won't need Charlie, Chris or even your mother taking care of you. I intend to do that myself."

"Why?" she asked once more, then added a little resentfully. "You didn't want me helping you out."

How to make her understand? Hunter was not big on baring his heart, but if ever there was a moment for truth, this was it. "You've been a caretaker for so long, it's second nature to you. In fact, it's a burden. I don't want to be another duty or a pity project. I'm stumbling along as I find my way with the kids, but I am finding it, Johanna." Okay, so here it came. "I want, no, I need to look after you while you're ill. Not out of some misguided sense of duty but because that's how it should be when you love somebody. You should want to care for them." Hunter took a deep breath. "And I do. Love you."

Johanna pulled her head away from his chest and looked into his eyes. She could see the truth shining there. "You didn't start dating me to get a mother for the kids, did you?"

Hunter blew out a breath. He didn't want any lies between them. "Yes. Yes, I did. But I was also attracted to you. And anyway, something happened along the way. I fell in love with you, Johanna. With *you*. Not some idea of an extra hand in running the carpools and packing the lunches.''

"I believe you." And she did. "And I've had a lot of time to think since you shut the door in my face last night."

"I didn't shut the door in your face."

"You did, too." Johanna held up her hand to stop any budding argument. "With all that thinking came some self-realization. You want to hear about it or not?"

"I'm not sure. Yeah, I guess."

"Okay then. I was really hurt that you wouldn't let me help you yesterday and I couldn't figure out why. I should have felt relief that you'd left me off the hook, right? Well I didn't. I was mad. And angry. And hurt. You want to know why? Because it wasn't another obligation, it wasn't something I assumed out of pity for your circumstances. It was because I loved you. The kids, too. They're a part of your package. And like you said, people who love *want* to help out. Because they care.''

The bathroom was quiet for several moments while Hunter sat on the closed toilet holding Johanna. The humidity from the tub had finished steaming over the room's mirror when he finally spoke. "Johanna, I know I'm asking a lot. I'm asking you to give up some of the freedom you've looked forward to for the last several years of your life, but will you marry me?"

Johanna didn't even have to think about it. "Yes."

Hunter reached up into the medicine cabinet over the sink and pulled down an unopened bottle of antihistamine lotion. He cracked the seal and unscrewed the cap, which left a small white ring of plastic at the mouth of the bottle. He pried the ring off the bottle and slipped it on the fourth finger of her left hand while Johanna watched with serious eyes.

"This will have to do until we can get to a jeweler."

"That could be another month of Sundays."

"Yeah, I know. You've got a splotch developing on your forehead."

Johanna rolled her eyes. "Thank you so much, Mr. Romance."

"You want romance? How about this?" And Hunter cradled her head in both of his big hands and just about kissed her blind.

Returning the kiss with equal fervor, Johanna finally let her mouth fall away. "I think my temperature just went up about ten degrees."

"You're burning me right through my shirt and jeans," Hunter agreed. "I need to get out of here." He shoved a box of baking soda at her. "Here. Soak. Get well. Quickly. I can't wait much longer."

Johanna scrambled off his lap, laughing. Laughing and looking at her plastic-bottle engagement ring with delight. She dumped the entire box into the tub. She would hurry and get well. She couldn't wait much longer, either.

* * * * *

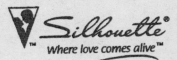

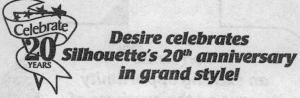

**Don't miss
an exciting opportunity
to save on the purchase of
Harlequin and Silhouette books!**

Buy any two Harlequin or
Silhouette books and save
$10.00 off future Harlequin
and Silhouette purchases

OR

buy any three
Harlequin or Silhouette books
and save **$20.00 off** future
Harlequin and Silhouette purchases.

*Watch for details
coming in October 2000!*

PHQ400

COMING NEXT MONTH